What if he'd

Matt daydreamed [...] happened if he'd pushed Susannah's jacket off of her slender shoulders and opened the little pearl buttons on that lacy blouse. If he'd stripped her down to nothing but those elegant high-buttoned boots and a rosy blush.

Would she have objected? Pushed him away and slapped his face? Or would she have clutched at his bare flesh as fervently as she'd clutched his lapels? Would she have melted against him, opening her body for his possession the way she'd opened her lips to his tongue?

The need to know was rapidly becoming an obsession.

He couldn't afford obsessions. No ambitious lawyer could.

And yet, here he was, obsessing. Wondering. Fantasizing.

And to hell with what it could do to his career.

THE PERSONAL TOUCH

BY

CANDACE SCHULER

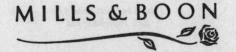

MILLS & BOON

MILLS & BOON and the Rose Device are trademarks of the publisher. TEMPTATION is a trademark of Harlequin Enterprises Limited, used under licence.
This edition published by arrangement with Harlequin Enterprises B.V.
First published in Great Britain in 1995
by Harlequin Mills & Boon Limited, Eton House, 18-24 Paradise Road, Richmond, Surrey TW9 1SR

© Candace Schuler 1994

ISBN 0 263 79103 3

21 - 9503

Printed in Great Britain by
BPC Paperbacks Ltd

1

MATTHEW RYAN GLANCED at the thin gold watch on his wrist for the third time since he'd folded himself into the yellow shantung wing chair. Then he looked up over the newspaper he held, frowning at the elaborately carved wooden door almost directly across from where he sat. The soft-voiced receptionist had warned him it would be a few minutes before Ms. Bennington could see him, but those few minutes had come and gone several times and the lady still hadn't appeared.

He'd had time to catalog the room's entire furnishings twice over, from the brass candlesticks and fresh freesias on the polished oak mantel, to the gently faded Brussels carpet beneath his feet, to the jewel-colored Tiffany lamp on the receptionist's desk. It was a warm, charming room, more like his mother's elegant front parlor than the reception area of a business establishment, he thought. Which wasn't really surprising, considering the offices of The Personal Touch were located on the ground floor of a stately old Victorian house in the trendy Pacific Heights district of San Francisco. Charming or not, though, Matt had seen all of it he wanted to see in the last fifteen minutes.

He closed the *Chronicle* with a snap, folding it into a neat, narrow rectangle without finishing the column he'd started to read, and laid it on the gleaming surface of the cabriolet table next to his chair. He'd give her five more minutes, he decided, and then he was leaving. He probably shouldn't have come in the first place, anyway. Especially without an appointment. But, dammit, he was just about at his wit's end.

His mother was driving him crazy.

Not that she wasn't a wonderful woman. She was. One of the best. It was just that she needed something—*someone*—other than her only son to fuss over now that she'd finally come to terms with her widowhood and joined the world again.

This morning, when a colleague in the D.A.'s office mentioned that his seventy-six-year-old father had used The Personal Touch and was as pleased as punch with the woman he'd been introduced to through it... Well, it had seemed like a good idea at the time.

"It's not your usual dating service," Cal had said just before court convened. "No slick pick-a-date videos or computer listings. None of that 'what's your favorite position from *The Kama Sutra*' stuff. It's more like an old-fashioned matchmaking service. You know, like that woman in *Fiddler on the Roof*? The one who arranged marriages for the villagers? This woman actually gives tea parties to introduce people to each other instead of letting them meet on their own in a bar somewhere. My dad really liked that aspect of it. Said he didn't feel like as big a fool as he would've otherwise."

After Matt thought about it a bit, mulling it over in the back of his mind while he listened to the opposing attorney argue for a continuance, it had still seemed like a good idea. When the judge had unexpectedly granted the defense's request, leaving Matt with the morning free, he'd decided to give it a try. It couldn't do any harm. And, with any luck at all, he thought now, grinning slightly, his mother would never have to know he'd fixed her up.

If this matchmaker woman ever puts in an appearance, that is.

Matt shifted in his chair, crossing his right ankle over the precise crease in the left knee of his crisply pressed navy-blue slacks. The long, well-manicured fingers of one hand drummed silently on the folded newspaper. *Two more minutes,* he told himself, frowning at the receptionist's lowered head.

She looked up, as if sensing his impatience, and met his eyes. The soft smile she gave him was strangely seductive. "I'm sure it won't be more than a minute or two longer," she said, hooking a lock of shiny black hair behind her ear with the tip of one very long, very red fingernail before she turned her attention back to the computer keyboard and the instruction manual lying open on the desk in front of her.

Matt wondered how she managed to hit the right keys with such long nails. They looked lethal. In fact, he thought, idly studying her, she looked a bit lethal herself. Her glossy black hair was done in a sassy china-doll style, the deep bangs and short, chin-length cut calling attention to her dark, slanted eyes and exotic bone structure. Her makeup was expertly, if a little heavily, applied. Her trim black dress was simple, but too sophisticated for her years, which couldn't, he thought, number much more than twenty. It occurred to him that he'd seen her somewhere before. Around the courthouse, maybe? Or at campaign headquarters?

She'd known his name, calling him Mr. Ryan before he'd introduced himself. That wasn't unusual, of course. As a high-profile attorney with more than his share of headline-making cases, his picture was in the papers on a fairly regular basis. Two weeks ago, when he'd finally announced his candidacy for district judge, there'd been a small flurry of coverage, both in the newspapers and on the local TV stations—mostly because the seat he'd declared for had once been occupied by his father. That she recognized him wasn't really surprising . . . but he still had the nagging feeling he knew her from somewhere far different from where she was now. It annoyed him not to be able to place her.

She looked up again, obviously feeling his continuing stare. "Could I get you a magazine, Mr. Ryan?" she asked, giving him another one of those oddly seductive smiles. "Or a different paper? I'm sure there's a copy of *The Wall Street Journal* around here some—"

She broke off as the carved door to the inner office opened. With a smile and a nod toward the open door she turned back to the work spread out on her desk, leaving Matt to deal with the two women who hovered on the threshold. They were deep in conversation, oblivious to anyone else in the room. "Can you think of anything I might have forgotten?" Matt heard the older one say.

She was standing with her back to him, but he could tell she was exactly what his brief conversation with Cal Westlake had led him to expect. Reassuringly plump and grandmotherly, she wore a lavender print dress that pulled a bit across the ample spread of her hips. An off-white cardigan hung from her shoulders, the arms swinging free and empty, held in place, he was sure, by one of those clip-on sweater guards from the nineteen-fifties that seemed to be coming back into style. Her shoes were low-heeled, beige and sensible. Her short brown hair was liberally streaked with gray. She carried a small stack of file folders in the crook of one arm and there was a pencil stuck behind her left ear. Her movements as she spoke were quick and birdlike, full of the energy and enthusiasm of a robin going after its morning meal.

A real old-fashioned matchmaker, Matt thought, instantly pegging her as the kind of benign busybody who loved giving advice. A widow, he decided, with a passel of kids who had long ago grown up and away from her sphere of influence, forcing her to find other lives to influence. Having pigeonholed her to his satisfaction, he automatically shifted his gaze to the woman who stood beside her.

Her face was turned three-quarters toward him, her head tilted to the right as she focused on what the older woman was saying. She was in her early-to-mid-thirties, slender and delicately built. About five foot five inches tall, Matt decided, mentally measuring her against his own six feet, with the graceful, upright posture of a prima ballerina. She was wearing a long, pastel-flowered skirt in muted watercolor shades of green and blue. It fluttered above her ankles, covering the tops of a pair of pale gray leather boots with small heels and a row of shiny round buttons up the sides. The boots were old-fashioned and oddly elegant, like something a woman might have worn at the turn of the century. The wide, lacy collar of a white linen blouse was spread out over the lapels of what looked to him like a man's sport coat. A tweedy mix of gray and pale moss green, it was just slightly too big, giving her a vaguely waiflike appearance despite her regal bearing. There was a lace hankie peeking out of the breast pocket and she had a fresh flower—gardenia, he thought—pinned on her left shoulder.

In keeping with the offbeat femininity of her clothing, her hair was long, unbound and wildly curly. It swirled around her shoulders in tempting disarray, its rich auburn color catching and reflecting the sunlight coming in through the lace curtains at the bay window. Her face was expressive and vividly alive, the wide mouth smiling and pursing, the strong auburn eyebrows lifting, then drawing together with apparent disregard for the formation of wrinkles as she responded to the older woman's comments. *A little unconventional*, Matt decided, pondering the dichotomy of the boxy man's jacket and the long flowing skirt, *but, all in all, a very appealing woman*.

He rose to his feet as the low-voiced conversation began to wind down, wondering why a woman with all she obviously had going for her would need the services of a matchmaker. "Ms. Bennington?" he said politely, addressing the older woman as he approached the pair.

It was the younger one who turned to look at him. "Yes?"

Matt's eyes widened a fraction. "Like that woman in *Fiddler on the Roof*," Cal had said when he'd recommended her. Matt wondered if Cal had had his eyes checked recently. "Susannah Bennington?" he said, just to be sure.

She smiled. "Yes," she said, her low voice laced with warmth and good humor. "I'm Susannah Bennington. May I help you, Mr. . . . ?"

"Ryan." He held out his hand. "Matthew Ryan."

Susannah put hers into it. "Of course. I should have recognized you from your pictures in the paper, Mr. Ryan."

"Matt," he said easily, returning the firm pressure of her handshake with unconscious care for the fragility of her delicate bones.

"Matt," she agreed with a slight nod. Her smile widened, deepening the dimples in either cheek. "You might be interested to know I'm seriously considering voting for you in November."

"I appreciate that." His answering smile softened his sharp, Nordic-blond good looks, giving him an appealing touch of vulnerability. "I need all the votes I can get."

"Oh." Susannah tilted her head assessingly, causing a stray curl to tumble over her forehead. She reached up, absently brushing it back with her free hand. "I think you'll get more than enough votes even without mine." She was sure half of San Francisco—male as well as female—could probably be counted on to vote for him on the basis of his face alone.

And if his looks didn't get them, his voice would. It oozed sexiness and authority in equal measures. Combine those two things—his looks and his voice—with his squeaky-clean record and the fact that he rarely lost a case, and you had a surefire winner in any political campaign. And despite the aw-shucks smile and self-effacing manner, she was sure he knew it. Men as good-looking and accomplished as Matthew Ryan always knew it.

"Is that why you're here?" she asked, withdrawing her hand from the suddenly uncomfortable warmth of his. "Is this an official campaign visit?"

"No, not at all. It's a—" he cast a significant glance toward the interior of her office and then looked back down at her "—private matter."

Susannah's expressive eyebrows rose. A private matter, was it? There was usually only one kind of private matter people brought to the door of The Personal Touch. But why would Matthew Ryan, a popular political candidate with a to-die-for body, leading-man looks and a blue-blooded background, need *her* to find a date? She would have thought a man like him would have droves of willing women throwing themselves at his expensively shod feet.

"Perhaps you'd better step into my office," she said, moving back to allow him to do so.

"Will that be all, Susannah?" the older woman asked as they turned toward the office.

"What?" Susannah looked around. "Oh, yes, thank you, Helen. That will be all for now. We'll go over the guest list for this week's party when you get back from lunch."

Helen Sanford nodded and, with a sharp look at Matthew, moved toward the receptionist's desk.

Matt slanted a glance at Susannah. "Was it something I said?" he asked quietly. The woman had looked at him as if he were a cockroach that had crawled across the toe of her sensible beige shoe.

Susannah shook her head. "It's nothing personal," she assured him, a rueful expression on her face as she watched the older woman walk away from them. Six months ago, Helen's husband of nearly thirty years had left her for a much younger woman; she'd been suspicious and distrusting of the entire male sex ever since. So far, none of Susannah's heart-to-hearts about the wisdom of letting go of her anger had done any good. Helen was eaten up with bitterness and—

"Ms. Bennington?"

Susannah brought her glance back to her prospective client's face. "I'm sorry," she murmured, tacitly apologizing for her wandering attention. Her smile flickered briefly, warm and unconsciously inviting. "And it's Susannah." She lifted her hand, graciously ushering Matt into her office ahead of her. "Shall we?"

He started to step past her and then paused, reaching out to put his hand on her arm instead, halting them both in the open doorway. Susannah looked up at him, an expression of mild inquiry on her face. Matt's gaze met hers head-on, from a distance that could be measured in inches.

He completely forgot what he'd been going to say.

Her eyes were brown. Not an ordinary run-of-the-mill brown, he thought as he stood there staring into them, nothing so mundane as that. They were a beguiling brown; a soft, rich velvety brown; as sweet and tempting as hot fudge; as full of warmth and sparkle as the finest aged brandy. The expression in them as she gazed up at him was open, inquisitive and expectant, clearly waiting for him to make his wishes known. Her full lips were slightly parted, as if she were ready to answer whatever question he might ask. He wondered what she would do if he bent his head and kissed her. Would the warmth in those soft brown eyes change to fire? Would those full, rosy lips part even more, answering his kiss with one of her own?

He has the clearest blue eyes I've ever seen, Susannah was thinking as she returned his penetrating stare. Clear, pure blue, like the icy-hot center of a flame or the heart of a priceless sapphire. They were intense. Focused. Predatory. She took an instinctive step back and came up against the doorjamb.

"Mr. Ryan?" She had to take a quick breath before she could continue. "Did you have a question?" she asked, more sharply than she had intended. "Mr. Ryan. Ah...Matt?"

Matt blinked. And then blinked again, forcing himself to remember where he was and what he'd been going to say. Freed from the mesmerizing spell of her gaze, he felt his good sense return the crazy impulse to kiss her passing as quickly as it had come. Almost. He removed his hand from her arm and moved past her into her office in an effort to put some distance between them.

"I've heard your service is very good. Very..." he hesitated tellingly over the word, "...discreet." His expression was rife with the significance of words unspoken. "Discretion is extremely important to me."

Susannah straightened away from the doorjamb and followed him into the office "No one will know you came to The Personal Touch unless you tell them," she said dryly, knowing perfectly well what he was getting at.

No wonder he'd been looking at her so searchingly, she thought, relieved to have a plausible reason for his intense regard of a moment ago. No political candidate alive would want it known that he'd had to resort to a dating service; the newspapers would be on the story like hungry ducks on a fat, juicy water beetle.

She turned and closed the door behind her, then motioned him toward the faded green velvet love seat situated between the bay window and her desk. "Please, make yourself comfortable," she invited, her voice and manner all business. "Would you like coffee or tea before we get started? A soft drink?"

Matt shook his head. "Now that I'm here I'd like to get this over with as quickly as possible." He glanced at his watch as he spoke. "I really haven't got any time to waste."

Which, Susannah thought as she moved behind her desk, probably answered her unasked question about why a man like him was in her office. Time. It was the constant lament of the modern, career-driven single; not enough time to devote to the task of finding someone to share an evening with, let alone a life. And a political candidate's life was undoubtedly busier than most, especially when it was added to the heavy caseload of a highly successful assistant DA.

She sat down. "Well, then, let's get right down to it, shall we?" She reached for a pen with one hand and pulled a lined yellow pad toward her with the other. "What are your requirements?"

"Requirements?"

"What kind of person are you looking for?"

Matt didn't even have to think about it. "Someone who would be a good companion," he said.

His answer surprised her. She'd been expecting him to begin with a description of the physical attributes he required in a woman. That was where most men started.

"Well-educated or at least well-read," he added, when she didn't say anything. "Someone who's interested in current events, who likes music and books and the ballet. Someone refined and—" he paused, looking for just the right word "—well-bred."

"Refined and well-bred," she said, nodding sagely as she scribbled on the pad in front of her. No wonder all those eager women throwing themselves at his polished calfskin wing tips weren't having any luck. *Wants a lady,* she wrote, her brows drawn together in a frown as she bracketed the last word in heavy quotes.

"Is that a problem?"

Only because it eliminates me as a candidate, Susannah thought before she could stop herself. She shook her head, both at him and herself. She wasn't in the market for a man, especially not one who wanted a woman to conform to the narrowly defined role of *lady.* Even if he did have the sexiest voice and the clearest blue eyes she'd ever encountered.

"What you're saying is that you want someone who could fit easily into San Francisco society," she said briskly, determined to push all thoughts of his admittedly impressive attractions aside. "Right?"

"Yes. Exactly," Matt said, relieved that she understood him so perfectly.

"What about hobbies? Any special interests besides the ballet?"

"The opera and symphony. Golf. Gardening." He thought about it for a second or two. "Some knowledge of roses would be a nice plus."

"Roses?" Susannah murmured, trying to imagine Matthew Ryan, cutthroat trial lawyer, with pruning shears in one hand and a basket of fresh-cut roses in the other. The image wouldn't quite come into focus.

"My mother's famous for her roses," he explained.

"Ah," she murmured knowingly. *A thoughtful son,* she wrote. *Wants a woman who will get along with his mother. Could be ready to get serious about someone.* She brushed away the niggling feeling of displeasure the thought gave her and added an exclamation point for emphasis. People who were ready to settle down were her favorite type of clients; it was so satisfying when she finally matched them up. "I assume you're looking for someone with similar political leanings?" She tilted her head, looking at him from under a tumble of auburn curls and a delicately lifted eyebrow. "No bleeding-heart liberals need apply?"

"No rigid conservatives, either."

Her eyebrow rose higher, inviting him to elaborate.

"We Ryans aren't nearly as stiff-necked as most people think," he said, his gaze meeting hers across the width of the desk. He smiled. Warmly. Intimately. Instinctively reacting to the unconscious flirtatiousness in her manner. "Honest."

Their gazes held for a brief, breathless second. An answering smile hovered on Susannah's lips. And then she flushed and looked back down at the pad in front of her. "How about religion?" she asked, telling herself to ignore the way his smile made those sexy blue eyes of his crinkle up at the corners. *I am not interested!* "Is it an important issue?"

"Well . . ." Matt shifted in his seat and looked down at the toe of his shoe as if it were the most interesting thing in the room. *Stop thinking about kissing her*, he told himself sternly. *Just stop wondering what that luscious mouth of hers would taste like.* "My family is Lutheran and we go to church most Sundays but, no—" he shook his head slightly "—it isn't a major issue."

Susannah nodded her understanding. *Tolerant*, she wrote.

"As long as we aren't talking practicing pagans or anything else too far from the mainstream," he added.

Up to a point, she noted.

"Do you have any special physical requirements?" she asked, telling herself that her interest in his answer was strictly professional.

"Physical requirements?" Matt asked.

"Height? Weight? Measurements? Complexion? Hair color? You know—" she risked a quick glance up at him without quite looking him in the eyes "—physical type?"

"Well, ah . . ." He hadn't given a thought to what his mother's physical type might be. His father had been a trim, fit man of average height with sandy brown hair and blue eyes. His most distinguishing feature had been the impassioned light blazing in those eyes whenever he talked about justice and the law. That, and the proud, upright way he'd carried himself until the series of strokes that finally took his life.

"I don't need a detailed list of specific characteristics," Susannah prompted. "Unless there's some physical attribute you feel is especially important. A certain minimum height, for example..." She let her voice trail off, hoping to encourage him to answer. Not that she expected a man like Matthew Ryan to actually get down to specifics like breast size or maximum allowable hip measurement the way some of her clients did. He was more sophisticated than that. "A general description is all I need," she said, her pen poised over the yellow pad, ready to take down all the polite euphemisms sophisticated men used for "built like a brick outhouse." Words like *tall, elegant, statuesque, blond...*

"Well, average height, I guess," Matt said at last, trying to picture his father in his mind. "Average weight. Not fat but not too skinny, either. And definitely not muscle-bound." He grimaced slightly. "You know the type I mean? The ones who look like they spend all day at the gym?"

"I think I know exactly what you mean," Susannah said, amazed and approving, hardly able to believe what she was hearing. *Might actually be interested in a real woman*, she wrote, and added two exclamation points. "Anything else?" She sneaked another quick peek at him from under her lashes as she asked the question.

Matt was still scowling at the toe of his shoe and missed her admiring look. "Neatly groomed," he said. His mother was fastidious about her own personal appearance. "And healthy," he added, thinking that it wouldn't do to have his mother's activities curtailed by someone who wasn't in good physical condition. She was very active for a woman her age.

Health conscious, she wrote. "Does that mean you'll be amenable to an AIDS test?"

That brought his head up. "An AIDS test?" Matt echoed disbelievingly. His mother, refined society matron, respected widow of a California supreme court justice, member of the San Francisco Garden Club, a sponsor of the Junior Symphony, his *mother*, take an AIDS test? The thought was ludicrous in the extreme. "An AIDS test won't be necessary," he said brusquely.

"Taking an AIDS test doesn't imply anything about anyone's morals or sexual orientation," Susannah said earnestly, looking up from the yellow pad to press her point. "In this day and age, it's simply a wise precaution any prudent person should take before embarking on a, ah..."

Their eyes met again, despite their best efforts not to let it happen. Unwanted awareness sizzled between them, skittering along their nerve endings like drops of icy-cold water on a red-hot griddle.

Matt shifted on the faded green love seat.

Susannah caught her breath.

But neither one of them looked away this time.

"...on a new, ah..." Susannah said, trying desperately to control her train of thought. She had this discussion with most of her clients sooner or later; it was nothing to get embarrassed about. Or excited about, either. *So why is my heart suddenly beating a mile a minute?* "A new..."

Matt leaned forward expectantly as her lips shaped the words, his long, lean body as tense as if he were awaiting the verdict in a precedent-setting trial.

"...sexual relationship," she finished breathlessly and waited, her gaze locked on his, for what would happen next.

They stared at each other for a heartbeat's worth of time that seemed to last for an aeon. Diamond-bright blue eyes bored into melting brown ones. Tempted and tempting. Speculating. Wondering. Fantasizing. Wanting. Denying.

I haven't got time for this, Matt told himself sternly. *Not on top of everything else I've got on my plate right now. And, besides, she's not even really my type.*

He's a client, Susannah reminded herself. *It would be unethical to get involved with a client. And he's not really my type, anyway.*

They both looked away.

"An AIDS test won't be necessary," Matt repeated firmly. He leaned back against the love seat and carefully picked a nonexistent piece of lint off the knee of his immaculate navy-blue slacks to avoid looking at her.

Susannah abandoned her attempt to convince him of the wisdom of an AIDS test, abruptly deciding he was perfectly capable of making his own decisions regarding his health. "Any preference as to hair color?" she asked, her head lowered, her gaze glued to the yellow legal pad in front of her.

"As long as it's not pink or purple or something crazy like that, it doesn't matter," he said shortly, eager to have this interview over and done with. "Eyes, either," he added, anticipating her next question. "I'd just like to find someone who's presentable and pleasant."

"How do you feel about smoking?"

"Nonsmoker, definitely."

"Drinking?"

"In moderation."

"Age range?"

"Ah...fifty-five to sixty-five." His mother was fifty-eight; his father had been sixty-two when he died.

That startled Susannah into lifting her head again. "Fifty-five to sixty-five?" she echoed, sure she couldn't possibly have heard him right.

"Maybe seventy," Matt allowed. "If he's a really young seventy."

"Seventy?" she said, incredulous. And then it hit her. Her eyes widened, her eyebrows rising into twin arches of disbelief and surprise. Had Matthew Ryan really said *he*?

"Susannah?"

2

HALF A DOZEN DISJOINTED thoughts tumbled through her mind in the next few seconds.

He can't be!

And even if he is, why would he want someone so much older than himself?

He must be absolutely crazy to risk his political career like this!

And even crazier to be so cavalier about the possibility of AIDS!

No wonder he wanted to speak to me in private!

No wonder he wasn't concerned with measurements!

And then, finally, from the deepest, most feminine recesses of her soul came the plaintive lament, *What a waste!*

Prodded by her silence, Matt looked up from his studied contemplation of the crease in his slacks. "I take it you think seventy is too old," he said when she just sat there with her pen poised above the yellow pad, staring at him with an odd expression on her face.

Susannah shook her head, wondering how on earth she could have misread him so completely. It wasn't as if he hadn't given her plenty of clues, she realized, both subtle and otherwise. Everything he'd said about an interest in the ballet and the opera being of primary importance...about roses and refinement...about the need for complete discretion. And the way he'd tried to avoid her gaze! It was all so clear. Now.

"Seventy isn't too old?"

"No, it's, ah . . ." She cleared her throat. "It's . . ."

"It's what?" he demanded, vaguely irritated by the way she just sat there, staring at him as if he'd suddenly grown a second head. "What's the matter?"

"Seventy's fine," she managed in a strangled voice. "If that's what you want, it's fine."

Matt snorted inelegantly. "Right," he said, pinning her with the look he used on uncooperative witnesses. "Now try the truth. What's the matter?"

She opened her mouth to answer him but nothing came out. What could she say? His sexual preferences were really none of her business. Except that it meant she needed to tell him The Personal Touch didn't handle same-sex pairings. Only how? In her nearly three years running a dating service, it had never come up before. Not once. She closed her mouth without saying a word.

"Susannah?"

"I just can't believe you're gay," she blurted, and then blushed beet-red.

Matt sat bolt upright on the love seat. *"What!"*

"I mean I *can* believe it, of course," she said, trying to cover the awkwardness of the moment with words, "because there you are, big as life. It's just that, when you first came in here, I didn't even begin to imagine you were." *Was it politically correct to say that?* "Not that there's any need to imagine it because lots of people are," she added, in case it wasn't. "Gay, that is. It's not as if it's unusual or anything. It's just that I assumed . . . I mean, you're just so hand—" *No, that was definitely an unenlightened thing to say! And stupid, too. Looks had nothing to do with it.* "You're in the newspapers so often and I've never heard any rumors or anything. And the way you looked at me . . . I mean," she corrected herself, "the way I *thought* you looked at me." She lifted her shoulders in a self-deprecating little shrug and tried to smile. The attempt was more than a little sheepish. "I didn't think you were, is all. I'm sorry if I've embarrassed you." *And myself*, she thought, cringing inwardly at the memory of the way she'd . . . well, ogled him when he obviously didn't want to be ogled. By a woman, anyway.

"Gay?" he said, just to be sure.

Susannah nodded.

Matt didn't know whether to be angry or insulted or . . . what. His first instinct was to leap across the desk and prove her wrong in some irrefutable and satisfyingly physical way. But Matt rarely went with his first instincts; his analytical lawyer's mind was too disciplined for that. Still, the urge to commit some overwhelmingly macho act in his own defense was undeniably there.

No one had ever questioned his sexual orientation before. He was utterly amazed that anyone would question it at all, ever. Especially a woman for whom he'd developed a rapidly escalating case of the hots from practically the moment he'd laid eyes on her. It was almost funny. Almost.

He stared at her for a moment, his expression revealing none of what he was feeling; neither the inchoate sense of masculine outrage nor the nascent urge to laugh. He relaxed against the back of the love seat, deliberately making his body language less threatening and accusatory. Any defense lawyer who'd ever faced him in a courtroom would have shuddered and said he was getting ready to rip a witness apart in cross-examination. "What led you to believe I'm gay?" he asked blandly.

"Well, actually, I didn't at first," Susannah admitted, sure he must already know that much. "Not until you said you didn't care if *he* was seventy, as long as *he* was a young seventy. I'm embarrassed to admit it but I actually thought you were talking about a woman up until that point." Her eyes meet his, wide and guileless, her expression mildly scandalized despite her attempt at sophisticated acceptance of an alternate lifestyle.

Matt felt his lips twitch with the need to smile. He ruthlessly quelled the need and continued to gaze at her, silently calling forth more information.

"I didn't realize you were describing your ideal man." Her tone was faintly accusing, as if she suspected him of having misled her on purpose.

With a strangled sound, somewhere between a groan and a snort of smothered laughter, Matt's sense of outraged masculinity finally succumbed to the absurdity of the situation. The really funny part, he thought, was that she was absolutely right. He *had* been describing the ideal man.

"For my mother," he said, still struggling to hide his smile.

The woman who had innocently impugned his manhood stared at him as if he'd gone crazy. "Your mother?"

"I was describing a man for my mother."

She stared at him blankly, unable to put what he'd just said together with what had gone before.

"To *date* my mother," Matt clarified, his piercing blue eyes dancing with barely suppressed merriment. "She's a widow."

"To date your..." Comprehension dawned. "Oh, good Lord." The rosy color in her cheeks, which had faded somewhat in the last few moments, bloomed into full color again. "Your mother." He was here to find a date for his *mother* and she'd accused him of being— Aghast at her faux pas, she covered her burning cheeks with both hands and stared at him over them. "Oh, good Lord," she said again, unable to think of anything more apropos to the situation.

Matt's hidden smile curved into a full-fledged grin. "Yes, I'd say that just about covers it," he agreed, enjoying her flustered consternation.

Susannah stared back at him for a second longer, taking in his grin and the amusement lurking in his eyes. Her hands dropped back down to the desk. "You're not angry," she said wonderingly, hardly able to believe it. Most heterosexual males of her acquaintance would be furious—or, at least, highly insulted by her assumption.

"I'm crushed," he said, clearly not crushed at all. "My ego may never recover from the blow."

Susannah couldn't stop her lips from curving up into a small answering smile. "Somehow I doubt even a

Sherman tank could crush your ego," she said, her tone half-admiring. "But I'm really sorry, anyway." And vastly—*unaccountably*, she told herself—relieved. "I just assumed you were here to find a date for yourself. A quite natural assumption, under the circumstances," she added in her own defense.

"Oh, quite natural," he murmured, still grinning.

"And when you said *he*, well...." She lifted one hand, palm up. "What can I say?" Her smile widened to match his. "I jumped to an obviously erroneous conclusion."

"You didn't think it was so obvious a minute ago," Matt reminded her, unable to resist the urge to tease her. She blushed so beautifully, the rosy color staining her cheeks and throat before spreading downward under the lacy collar of her blouse. The expression in his eyes heated as he wondered just how far down the color went. Because she'd had the temerity to suspect him of being gay, he let the heat build. And made sure she felt it.

Susannah took a quick little breath. "Yes, well . . ." She flicked her hand, brushing the remark—and the heat—aside, and picked up her pen. "Shall we start over?" she said briskly, intent on putting the whole embarrassing episode behind her. "The notes I took—" she tapped the pad with the point of her pen "—aren't going to be very helpful the way they are."

"I'VE GOT TO WARN YOU, Matt, I've never worked this way before," Susannah said fifteen minutes later, after he'd told her what he felt were all the pertinent facts about his mother. "I've never matched up anyone without meeting both parties face-to-face first. Match-

making for me has always been much more than a
matter of pairing up lists of compatible likes and dis-
likes," she explained, indicating the notepad in front of
her. "I rely on my impressions and intuition about a
person, too."

"Intuition?" His smile was gently teasing, full of
masculine amusement. "You mean, like, feminine intuition?"

"Gut instinct. Hunch," Susannah said, refusing to
rise to the lure. "Whatever you want to call it. The point
is, on paper two people can appear to be as compatible
as twin peas in a pod and yet have absolutely no chem-
istry together. And, vice versa," she added, involun-
tarily thinking of her unwanted reaction to him. "Some
of my best matches have been between people who
didn't seem to have anything in common at all. But they
hit it off instantly."

"I'm sure you'll manage to come up with someone
who'll be just fine."

"Even if I do come up with a suitable candidate, I
don't see how I'm going to get him together with your
mother unless she knows what's going on."

"Don't worry about that part of it," Matt said. "You
just find the right guy. Getting them together is my department."

"And you've already got that department organized. Right?"

"Of course." Matt's nod was the epitome of assured
self-confidence. "Easiest thing in the world to introduce him to her during my next campaign appearance
or at some benefit or other. As long as he's discreet—"

and Matt's tone said he'd better be " —she'll never suspect a thing."

"So why haven't you done it before now?"

Matt lifted an eyebrow. "Come to a dating service?"

"Fixed her up. You must know lots of eligible men. Lawyers. Judges. Captains of industry." Her tone was gently mocking. "Pillars of the community. Political bigwigs."

"I've tried." Matt sighed. "Believe me, I've tried. But all the eligible men I know, she knows. And has known for years. Most of them either worked with or were friends of my father's before he died. If she had any interest in any of them, don't you think it would have manifested itself by now?" He shook his head. "I know when I've exhausted my options." He smiled appealingly and spread his hands. "And when it's time to call in the professionals."

"Well, speaking as a professional, I think you should tell your mother what you're up to. It seems . . . I don't know—" Susannah shrugged "—dishonest to do it behind her back. Especially if she hits it off with whoever. It'd be like starting off a relationship with a lie. Not a good idea," she warned him.

"It's just a tiny little white lie. And it's the only way my mother's going to be open to meeting anyone new."

"But—"

"Like I said, I've already tried fixing her up but she refuses to cooperate. She says she's 'past all that nonsense.' I suspect what she really means is that she wouldn't feel comfortable dating any of my dad's old friends."

"Maybe she's still mourning your father," Susannah suggested gently. "Two years isn't really all that long to grieve."

Matt sighed. "I think a part of her will always grieve for my father—they'd celebrated their thirty-seventh anniversary just before he had his first stroke—but the signs that she's finally gotten over the worst of it are there, believe me. She's begun to take a real interest in life again." In *his* life, especially, and most especially his recently announced bid for district judge. "She's ready to go on to the next stage, whatever it is." His grin flashed briefly. "God knows, I'm ready for her to go on to the next stage."

"Well, I'll give it my best shot but I can't prom—" The phone rang shrilly, cutting her off in midsentence. She glanced at it, waiting for the light to go on that would tell her it had been picked up by one of the women in the outer office. It rang twice more before she excused herself to Matt and reached for the receiver.

"The Personal Touch," she said pleasantly. "How may I help you?" She listened a moment. "I'm sorry, sir, we don't match people up over the telephone. You'll need to come in for an inter—" A frown drew her brows together as she listened to the caller restate his request. "You've obviously made a mistake," she said, icicles dripping from every word. "We're not that kind of dating service. No," she said firmly, when the caller tried to argue. "I haven't misunderstood anything. You have. This isn't some trashy escort service with hourly rates."

Matt lifted an eyebrow at her as she replaced the receiver.

"Some men seem to think *dating service* is a euphemism for *call-girl service*," she said with a grimace of distaste.

At her words, a light went on in Matt's mind. "Your receptionist," he said, suddenly picturing the sleek, seductive young woman he'd seen in the outer office in a far different setting.

"I beg your pardon?"

"I knew I'd seen her somewhere before, but I couldn't place her until just now. She's been in court more than once." His gaze was steady and speculative. "Are you aware that your receptionist is a prostitute?"

"Ex-prostitute," Susannah corrected him calmly. "She hasn't been out on the streets for almost a year."

The lawyer in him had formed his next question before he even thought about it. "Do you know that for a fact?"

"Yes, I do. Judy's been working for me part-time since she quit the streets. Her parole officer is an old friend of mine," she added, feeling compelled to explain.

"Only part-time?"

"She goes to secretarial school the rest of the time," Susannah said, her voice edging toward cool. "And I resent your implication."

Matt ignored the warning. "If I remember her case rightly," he said, and he remembered just about every case that had ever crossed his desk, "she's got a string of arrests going back, oh, a good seven years, at least. And not just prostitution. She's done time for drug possession and petty theft, too."

"I'm aware of that." Susannah's tone slipped from cool to frosty. "What's your point?"

Matt inclined his head toward the phone. "You don't think she had anything to do with that?"

"No," Susannah said firmly. "I don't."

"Don't you think you should consider the possibility?"

"The Personal Touch has received the occasional call like that practically since the day we opened for business." There was almost as much ice in her tone now as there had been when she was talking to the caller. "Well *before* Judy started working here. As I said, some men think the terms *dating service* and *call girl* are interchangeable." She stood up, deliberately signaling the end of the interview.

Matt remained seated. "Seems to me working part-time for a dating service might be an excellent cover for other, shall we say, less savory activities."

Susannah abruptly wondered how she could have ever thought him attractive, or even considered voting for him. The man was obviously a hard-nosed, hard-hearted hard-liner without an ounce of compassion or understanding in his whole gorgeous body. "It must be very difficult, going through life burdened with all that suspicion and self-righteousness."

"I'm an attorney with the DA.'s office," he said easily, refusing to be baited. "It's my job to be suspicious."

"And the smug self-righteousness? Is that part of your job, too?"

Matt found it just a bit harder to reply calmly this time. "I prefer to think of it as common sense," he said, surprised that such a relatively mild jibe had gotten under his skin. He'd been accused of much worse in the course of his career and been able to brush it off with an unconcerned shrug. But this woman seemed to have a real knack for riling him. "Habitual criminals rarely turn into model, law-abiding citizens," he said sharply. "Especially not overnight."

"Judy Sukura is not a criminal, habitual or otherwise," Susannah said heatedly, all trace of coolness disappearing from her voice and manner. "She's a young woman who was given a very raw deal in life. She's been physically and sexually abused, both at home and on the streets, and she's dealt with it the best way she could, doing what she thought she had to to survive. And, for your information, *Counselor*—" the inflection she gave the word made it sound like a particularly virulent disease "—she didn't make some miraculous, overnight change. It's taken months of therapy and hard work and plain, gut-wrenching effort for her to get to where she is today. And it's going to take a lot more of the same before she can completely overcome the abuses of her past, including, I might add, those inflicted by the callous, uncaring maze we call a legal system, which treats women like Judy as if they were dangerous criminals instead of giving them the help and understanding they so desperately need."

She stopped and took a deep breath, forcibly bringing herself under control. "So, you can just take your nasty little suspicions and your self-righteous smugness right on out of here. Now." She gave him a heated glare, full of simmering indignation on behalf of her receptionist. "I don't have the time or the inclination to deal with some tight-ass assistant district attorney with more ambition than compassion."

Five seconds of utter silence greeted her tirade.

"Ex-social worker, right?" Matt asked.

Susannah gaped at him for a moment. "What?"

"That bit about 'the callous, uncaring maze we call a legal system,'" he said, a touch of asperity in his tone. He was getting really tired of all the abuse heaped on lawyers lately. And of people who thought anything the government had a hand in was automatically suspect. "Either you used to work within that system and burned out, or you feel you were worked over by it," he said, watching her for a reaction. "I'd go with the first." She didn't strike him as someone who had been through the system herself, although you never knew; there was enough anger there for her to have been a recipient of the government's slow-moving, unsentimental largess. He leveled an uncompromising, implacable look at her over the desk. "State, county or city?"

"County Social Services," she said before she could think not to. There was something about the way he asked that compelled her to answer.

He brushed aside the spurt of satisfaction being right gave him and pushed for more information. "How long?"

"Almost five years. Five frustrating, infuriating years," she added before he could ask. "And, yes, I burned out, as you so eloquently put it." It was still a sore spot with her, that she hadn't had whatever it took to hang in there for the long haul. "It finally got to the point where I couldn't take it anymore and I quit," she said baldly, daring him to make something of it.

His lifted eyebrow managed to look mocking. "It?"

"The endless red tape and paperwork, the long hours, the bureaucratic lack of compassion for the very people I was supposed to be helping. I got tired of spinning my wheels and going nowhere."

He gave her a deliberately disparaging look. "And so now you're safely out of it and you think the system and the people in it stink."

"No, not the people," she said indignantly. "Most of the people who work in Social Services are hardworking and well-intentioned—" *at least, at first, before the hopelessness of it gets them down* "—doing the best they can with what they have to work with. But the system . . . ?" She paused, afraid of offending him, and then decided to just go ahead and say it. He hadn't appeared to worry in the least about offending her. And it was, after all, what she truly believed. "Definitely, yes," she said with an emphatic nod. "I think the system pretty much stinks. It has too many loopholes and lets too many people fall through the cracks. People like Judy. And the homeless. And teenage runaways." Her hands fluttered up into the air as she got into it. "Battered women and children. AIDS patients. Disabled veterans. The impoverished elder—"

"So what are you doing to make it better?" Matt demanded, suddenly fed up with bleeding-heart liberals who whined about the way things were but didn't do a thing to try and make them better.

"What?"

"You stand there," he said, not bothering to hide his sarcasm, "bellyaching about all the ills of the present system. But instead of trying to improve it, you jumped ship. I want to know what you're doing to make things better."

"I was planning on voting for you," Susannah shot back, her tone equally sarcastic. "But now I'm not so sure!"

Her answer surprised them both and they stared at each other for a long moment, shocked at the excess of overheated emotion zinging back and forth between them.

"Good Lord," Susannah said, putting a hand to her throat in a vain effort to calm her runaway pulse. "How'd we get into this? No, never mind." She made a vague brushing-away motion. "Don't tell me. I don't want to know."

"Good. Because I don't think I know the answer," Matt admitted. "I'm not in the habit of..." He lifted his broad shoulders in a halfhearted shrug, feeling uncomfortably like a tongue-tied schoolboy who'd started a silly argument with the girl sitting next to him just to get her attention—and then didn't know what to do with it when he had it. "I don't usually fly off the handle like that," he finished.

"No. No, me either," Susannah said, instantly and instinctively understanding all that he wasn't saying. "Well, then..." She made a loose fist, bouncing it nervously against the notepad on her desk a couple of times as she searched her mind for something to say. "I guess that concludes our, um, business. I'll call you when I have someone lined up. That is—" she hesitated, recalling the words *tight-ass* and *bellyaching* "—if you still want me to?"

For just a second, Matt considered the wisdom of changing his mind. And then, inexplicably, he decided to ignore what was surely his better judgment. "I still want you to," he said with a brief nod.

"Okay, good," she said, too brightly. "That's good. I'll call you when I have someone lined up." She moved around the desk toward the door, unconsciously walking a little faster as he rose from the love seat to follow her. "We can decide what to do about setting up a meeting between them then."

She reached out with her right hand to open the door. He reached out with his left and covered hers on the old-fashioned brass doorknob.

"There's just one more thing," he said softly.

Susannah was afraid she knew exactly what that one thing was. Knew, too, that it was probably in her best interests to avoid it. But she made no move to do so.

"I probably won't have any candidates for you before next week at the earliest," she said, as if he hadn't spoken. As if he wasn't standing there with his hand on hers. As if she wasn't standing there, staring at it, transfixed.

It seemed huge, covering hers completely. His fingers were long and square-tipped, the nails clean and lightly buffed, the wrist thick and substantial beneath the snowy-white cuff of his shirt. Except for the neatly manicured nails, they could have been the hands of a laborer, tanned, strong and capable-looking. Susannah tried to tell herself she wasn't the least bit affected.

"It usually takes at least a week to find a suitable match," she said. "Maybe longer in your case since I—"

His fingers tightened on hers, just slightly, and he lifted her hand from the ornate doorknob.

"—since I haven't meet your mother one-on...ah..." her voice faltered as he pulled her to him "...one..." It died away completely when he cupped her cheeks in his wide palms and turned her face up to his.

Their eyes met for a fleeting second, long enough for her to see the searing heat and purpose in his. Long enough for him to glimpse the answering heat in hers. And then her lashes fluttered down and his lips took hers in a kiss more carnal than any first kiss should be.

His mouth was skillful and insistent against hers; rife with masculine hunger; blatantly masterful, allowing no room for argument or refusal. Susannah offered none, choosing instead to answer fire with fire. Her head fell back under the aggressive onslaught of his lips. Her mouth opened to accept his seeking tongue. Her hands clutched at the lapels of his navy-blue suit to hold him as securely as he was holding her. She stood toe-to-toe with him for hot, endless seconds, giving as good as she got, taking as much as she gave. When he finally lifted his head, he was breathing as heavily as she was.

And trying just as desperately not to show it.

Susannah gulped back a shuddering sigh and loosened her hands on his lapels. "Was there a point to that?" she asked with credible calm, just as if her head wasn't spinning. And her heart wasn't slamming against the inside of her chest. And she couldn't feel the rock-hard erection pressed against her stomach.

Matt let his hands drop from her face and stepped

back. "Just in case you had any lingering doubts," he
said raggedly, and let himself out of the office before he
did something *really* stupid like tearing her clothes off
and taking her down to the floor beneath him.

3

"HE'S THE THIRD DUD you've sent over."

Susannah frowned at the telephone. "None of those men are duds," she objected. "All three of them are very nice, conservative, well-bred—" *boring* "—gentlemen. Exactly the kind of man you said your mother would be interested in."

"Well, she wasn't," Matt complained. "She turned them all down flat. She hasn't been out on a single date yet."

"And who's fault is that? I told you I probably wouldn't be able to find someone suitable this way," she reminded him. "I need to meet her, Matt. There are things I can only tell about a person, *in* person. That's why I call this business The Personal Touch, you know. Because that's what successful matchmaking takes— personal one-on-one contact."

There was a long pause on the other end of the phone. "All right." He sighed. Loudly. "You can meet her."

"Oh, good," she said, pleased and relieved that he was finally willing to listen to reason. "The sooner the better. Let's see . . ." She flipped a page on her desk calendar as she spoke. "How about lunch tomorrow? She can come here or I can meet her at a restaurant. Unless

you think she'd be more comfortable being inter-
viewed at home? I don't usually do that but—"

"No."

"Not tomorrow?" She flipped more pages. "Well, the
rest of this week is booked pretty solid but I could—"

"I don't mean 'no, not tomorrow,'" Matt interrupted. "I mean 'no, you're not going to interview her.'"

"But you just said—"

"I said you could meet her. I didn't say you could tell
her I hired you to find her a date."

It was Susannah's turn to sigh. "Your mother's hardly
likely to tell me what I need to know unless she knows
why I'm asking. I don't think 'Hello, Mrs. Ryan, I'm so
pleased to meet you. Tell me, what do you look for in
a man?' is going to work. Not unless she's a lot different than you've led me to believe."

Which, Susannah reflected, she might very well be.
The woman Matt had described should have been
pleased as punch with any one of the first three candidates. That she hadn't been pointed to a serious flaw
in her son's powers of observation. Or, at the very least,
a blind spot where his mother was concerned.

"I think you should tell her what you're up to, Matt,"
she advised. "You never know. If she's as lonely for
companionship as you think, she might actually like the
idea."

"No." Matt was adamant on that point. "She
wouldn't. She's very old-school, very proper and dignified. In my mother's world, things are done a certain
way or they aren't done at all."

"All right," Susannah conceded, knowing her own
mother would feel exactly the same way. *Plebeian* was

one of the least scathing adjectives Audrey Stanhope Bennington Harper had used when Susannah announced she was going to turn her grandmother's legacy into a dating service. "When and where do I meet her?" She'd find *some* tactful way to elicit the necessary information.

"Are you free tonight?"

"Tonight? Well, let's see..." She hesitated, some primal feminine instinct warning her not to reveal just how empty her evenings were. She rifled through her calendar, making sure he could hear the rustle of the pages. "Yes, tonight's open," she said, making it sound as if it were a rare occurrence. The truth was, except for The Personal Touch's regular get-acquainted parties and the occasional night out with ex-colleagues from her old job at Social Services, almost every night was open.

"Good. I'll pick you up at six-thirty."

"Pick me up? There's no need to pick me up," Susannah protested. "Just tell me where and I'll—"

"I'll pick you up," Matt insisted. "My mother's having a few friends over for cocktails before they all head off to some concert at Davies Hall tonight. We'll tell her you're my date."

Susannah felt her stomach clench. "Date?" She couldn't remember the last time she'd been on an actual date. It had been at least a year. Maybe longer. And never with a man who could make her blush with just a look.

"You want to meet her one-on-one. Get to know her, don't you?"

"Well, yes, but—"

"This is perfect, then. As my date, you'll have ample opportunity to talk to her. Size her up. Whatever it is you need to do. In fact, just to make sure, we'll get there a little early. Give you some extra one-on-one time with her before everyone else arrives."

"But—"

"Can you be ready by six o'clock?"

Susannah knew she should say no. Gut instinct was telling her that spending any time at all with Matthew Ryan—even as his pretend date—was just asking for trouble. Big trouble. It had been a long time since a man's kiss had made her toes curl. *Like since never.* "Yes, six o'clock is fine," she said.

"Good. See you then. Ah..." He hesitated. "My mother dresses up for these things," he said delicately, not wanting to offend her. "Nothing formal. No long dresses or anything like that. Just..." *What did women call those kinds of clothes?* "...cocktaily kinds of dresses. Fancy but not too fancy." And nothing like that offbeat outfit she'd been wearing in her office. "Do you know the kind I mean?"

"I know," she said, wondering if she should feel insulted. She decided to let it pass. The poor man was the product of an environment where perfectly creased navy serge suits and spit-polished wing tips were considered to be on the cutting edge of fashion. "I have the perfect dress." She'd bought it for those times when she couldn't get out of some function her mother had invited her to. "I promise, you won't be embarrassed to be seen with me," she said dryly, unable to resist the dig.

"You misunderstand me," Matt said smoothly, as sincere as a politician making campaign promises—or a man trying to lull a woman into unsuspecting complacency. "I was just trying to explain that my mother has some old-fashioned ideas about things like dress and deportment. So much so that she even dresses for dinner at home alone. I never meant to imply anything about your taste. I'm sure nothing you'd wear could embarrass anyone," he added gallantly, hoping it was true.

"I wouldn't bet on it," Susannah mumbled. She'd embarrassed her mother more times than she could count. Sometimes deliberately.

"Beg pardon?"

"Nothing," Susannah said. "I'll see you at six."

MATT STARED at the phone for a long moment after he'd hung it up, wondering if he was out of his mind for thinking what he was thinking, planning what he was planning. The truth was, having Susannah meet his mother was only an excuse to see her again. One he'd been looking for since he'd walked out of her office two weeks ago with an ungodly ache between his thighs and the sweet taste of her burning on his lips.

He'd told himself that she wasn't the cool, sophisticated, demure type he usually preferred. He'd reminded himself that he didn't have the time right now for a relationship, even if she had been his usual type. He'd even tried imagining the fit his campaign manager would throw if he knew Matt was fantasizing about becoming involved with a bleeding-heart liberal who ran a dating service and employed an ex-hooker as a receptionist. Poor old Harry would have that coronary he was always threatening everybody with.

But none of his mental gymnastics had worked worth a damn.

For the past two weeks, despite the long list of reasons he gave himself for not thinking about her, Matt had found himself thinking about her anyway, even when he was supposed to be thinking about something else. It was an unprecedented first in his heretofore single-minded dedication to his career. A crack in his legendary ability to concentrate despite any and all distractions.

He'd found himself idly thumbing through a folder of legal briefs he should have been reading, wondering instead what would have happened if he'd let that kiss go on just a few moments longer. He'd listened to a colleague recount a brilliant closing argument and fantasized about how Susannah's breast would have felt in his hand. He'd pretended to be paying attention as Harry discussed the strategy for an upcoming political fund-raiser and daydreamed about what might have happened if he'd pushed that too-big jacket off of her slender shoulders and opened the little pearl buttons on that lacy blouse. If he'd unzipped that long flowing skirt and let it drop to the floor. If he'd stripped her down to nothing but those elegant high-buttoned boots and a rosy blush.

Would she have objected? Pushed him away and slapped his face? Or would she have clutched at his bare flesh as fervently as she'd clutched at his lapels? Would she have melted against him, opening her body for his possession the way she'd opened her lips to his tongue? And would he be remembering how good it had felt to be sheathed inside her heat and softness instead of wondering how it *might* feel?

The need to know was rapidly becoming an obsession.

And he couldn't afford obsessions. No political candidate could.

And, yet, here he sat, obsessing.

Wondering.

Fantasizing.

And to hell with what it could do to his campaign.

No, I don't mean that, he thought with a quick spurt of guilt. The campaign was important. His father had been a San Francisco district judge, holding the position for three terms before he was appointed to fill a seat on the California Supreme Court. Matt had always known he was destined to follow in his father's illustrious footsteps. It was what he'd been born to do, what he'd been groomed for, and why he'd initially chosen to study law.

If the chance to fulfill his destiny had come a bit sooner than he'd expected, well, that was politics. As Harry always said, you had to strike while the iron was hot. Two back-to-back convictions of local drug kingpins, plus the get-tough-on-crime mood of the voters, had made the iron very hot. He had to make his bid for district judge now, while he was San Francisco's favorite son. If he put it off or messed it up, the chance might not come again for a long time. Or ever.

Which was why he couldn't let himself be distracted by a woman who wasn't even his type in the first place. No, he decided, he'd see her again, take her out, then take her to bed as soon as she'd let him. At best, he'd be completely cured of his ridiculous obsession with her. At worst, once he knew what she felt like and tasted like, once the mystery was gone, he'd be able to get her out of his mind long enough to concentrate on the campaign.

"I'M GOING TO KNOCK OFF a little early," Susannah said as she stepped out of her office into the reception area.

Helen looked up from her seat at the receptionist's desk, quick concern clouding her brow. "Aren't you feeling well?"

"I'm feeling fine," Susannah assured her. *I'm having hot flashes and heart palpitations and I've probably lost my mind but I'm fine.* "I have to meet a client for an outside interview, and I want to freshen up and change clothes before I go." She glanced down the hallway toward the tiny under-the-stairs bathroom and then through the carved pocket doors that opened into the formal front parlor. "Has Judy left already?" The receptionist's Friday night computer class didn't start until six o'clock and she usually left right from the office. It was barely five o'clock.

"I sent her over to The Tea Cozy to get something to eat before she goes to class," Helen said. "She spent her lunch hour right here at this desk, studying for some test, and she was planning on skipping her dinner, too, until I threatened to go over there and bring her back something to eat myself." She shook her head, as if the workings of the younger woman's mind were a complete mystery to her. "One of these days that girl's going to end up fainting from hunger, right here in this office. Probably right in front of a client, too. A fine impression that would make, I told her," she grumbled, gruff as a mother hen. "Clients get upset when people faint in front of them. It's not good for business."

Susannah hid a smile. "I'm sure she'll be more careful in the future."

Helen's expression clearly said she'd believe that when she saw it. "If she's eating a good dinner like I told her to, she's probably still there. Did you want to talk to her about something? I could call over and check. Or run over and get her."

"No, thank you, Helen. I was just wondering out loud." Susannah wandered to the window as she spoke, reaching over to tweak one of the lace panels into more perfect alignment against the window frame. Her hand froze in midmotion. "Isn't that Eddie Devine?" she said, leaning forward to peer out the window.

"Who?"

"Eddie Devine. He's standing outside The Tea Cozy."

Helen came to the window to stand beside Susannah. "Who's Eddie Devine?" she asked.

"Oh, that's right. You don't know him." Susannah hesitated, unwilling to reveal too much of Judy's past. It was, after all, up to her to decide how much she did— or didn't—want people to know about her life. "Judy used to work for him," Susannah said obliquely, hoping to let it go at that.

Helen slanted a glance at her. "You mean he was her pimp?"

"She told you about it, then?"

"Some of it." Helen looked back out the window, her lips pursed up as if she'd just sucked on a lemon. "He

looks just like one of those slick hoodlums you see on
TV. All decked out in a loud, tacky silk shirt and gold
chains." She sniffed disdainfully. "I bet he uses mousse
on his hair." A man who used mousse was pond scum
in Helen's book; her husband had started using it just
before he left her for a younger woman. "What do you
suppose he's doing, hanging around here?"

"Nothing good," Susannah said. Her soft brown eyes
narrowed menacingly. "Maybe I should go out there
and tell him to get lost before Judy comes out of The Tea
Cozy. I'm sure it would upset her to see him."

Helen put her hand on Susannah's arm. "Too late,"
she said, and nodded toward the street. "There she is."

They stood behind the lace curtains, watching as
Judy came out of the pastel-colored Victorian building
that housed the trendy tea shop across the street from
The Personal Touch. She was distracted as she descended the front steps, not really watching where she
was going. Her head was bent, her fingers busy fid-
dling with the strap of the black leather tote bag dangling from her shoulder. She almost bumped into Eddie
as she stepped off the bottom step onto the sidewalk.
She looked up in surprise. Her face went white under
her carefully applied makeup.

Susannah watched her shrink back, cringing as her
former pimp reached out to touch her. He said something. Asked something. Judy shook her head and tried
to sidle around him. He moved closer, blocking her
way, obviously trying to intimidate her with his pres-
ence, talking all the while. She shook her head again,
more forcefully, and glanced across the street toward

The Personal Touch as if seeking refuge. Or taking courage.

Eddie grabbed her arm, forcibly reclaiming her attention.

She stiffened.

"No," she said, her lips clearly forming the word. "No."

And then she pulled her arm out of his hand and brushed past him, her head held high, her back stiff as she hurried toward the BART station at the far end of the street.

"Oh, good for you, Judy," Susannah said, as proud as if a child of hers had faced down the playground bully. "Good for you."

She continued watching as Judy disappeared into the crowd milling around the entrance to the subway station, ready to run outside and intervene if Eddie started to follow her. He appeared to think about it for a moment, scowling at Judy's retreating figure with a look of frustration and anger twisting his features. Then he swore and stalked over to the black Trans Am parked illegally at the curb. He revved the engine, leaving rubber on the road as he peeled away.

"Nasty character." Helen spat the words out as if they tasted bad.

"Yes," Susannah agreed, finally turning away from the window. "But, fortunately, he's not nearly as nasty or as tough as he thinks he is. He's small potatoes," she said when Helen's expression asked for further explanation. "A two-bit operator who's only good at intimidating frightened young women. And not even very good at that," she added with satisfaction, thinking of the way Judy had stood up to him.

"Do you think we should call the police or her parole officer or somebody?" Helen asked. "He might be trying to make her go back to work for him."

"I'm sure that's exactly what he had in mind," Susannah said. "But it looked as if Judy handled it just fine. She told him no and walked away."

"But what if he comes back?"

"If he does, we'll deal with it then. As I said, he's not nearly as tough as he'd like everyone to believe he is. So I think it's okay if we leave it alone for now," she said, knowing that doing so was bending the rules a bit.

Technically, any contact between a parolee and a former criminal associate was supposed to be reported to the supervising parole officer. In general, it was a good rule, made for a good reason. But there were also good reasons to break the rules now and then. Susannah knew in her heart that this was one of those reasons.

"Judy took a major step today in facing him down by herself," Susannah said, explaining her decision to Helen. "She hasn't done that before. I think it's important that she knows the victory is all hers, without outside help. And I don't think we should mention that—" she motioned toward the window, indicating the scene they had witnessed "—unless she brings it up herself. We don't want her to think we've been spying on her. Or that we don't trust her." She reached out and patted the older woman's shoulder. "Okay?"

Helen cast a last lingering glance at the curtains. "Okay," she agreed.

SUSANNAH'S CONSERVATIVE, knee-length, wool-crepe dress was black. Her stockings were black. Her small clutch purse was black. Her leather pumps, decorated with tiny ladylike bows at the vamp, were black. She wore pearl studs in her ears and a single sixteen-inch strand of pearls around her neck—both high school graduation gifts from her mother. A delicate gold watch with a face so tiny you almost needed a magnifying glass to read it encircled her left wrist—a gift from her seldom-seen father on the same occasion. The sweet, flowery perfume she wore had been given to her three years ago by a nice, boring man her mother still insisted would have made Susannah a perfect husband. Her makeup was so subdued as to be practically nonexistent. Her curly red hair had been ruthlessly smoothed back to the nape of her neck, coiled into the semblance of a bun and secured with a handful of hairpins, a liberal coating of hair spray and a flat grosgrain bow—also black.

Her father would have smiled absently and told her she looked like a perfect little lady. Her mother would have brushed back the tendrils of red hair that always escaped the hairpins and asked her why she didn't try to dress nicely more often. Matthew Ryan would probably think she looked sophisticated and chic.

Susannah grimaced at her reflection in the mirror. "You look like a Stepford wife on her way to a funeral," she said, disgusted that she had once again given in to expediency and donned the disguise needed to fit in to the conservative, rarified society into which she had been born.

Except that this was business, she reminded herself. It wasn't a date, no matter what Matt had called it. And in business, dressing to win approval didn't mean you'd caved in to the pressure to conform. No, indeed. Dressing for business meant you were smart enough to know that the way you looked was important. It was called 'dressing for success.' Men did it all the time. Why else would they put up with starched shirts, three-piece suits and neckties, if not in the name of commerce?

Susannah put a hand to her hair, tucking in an escaped tendril, then turned and got a traditional, double-breasted camel-hair coat—her reward for graduating from college—out of the closet. Even in mid-June, San Francisco nights could dip down into the low fifties. Shrugging into it, she switched off the bedroom light and headed downstairs, determined to be ready and waiting when Matt arrived to pick her up. The less like a date this *business* meeting was, she thought, the happier she would be.

MATT'S MOTHER was aristocratic, elegant and distinguished, with perfectly coiffed blond hair, a regal bearing and simple, classic taste in clothes. Her eyes were blue, like her son's. Her smile was warm and gracious.

"Mom, this is Susannah Bennington, a friend of mine." Matt performed the introductions as he helped Susannah out of her coat. "Susannah, my mother Millicent Ryan."

Susannah smiled and held out her hand, just barely managing to restrain the impulse to curtsy. "It's a pleasure to meet you, Mrs. Ryan."

Millicent Ryan returned the slight pressure of Susannah's fingers and murmured that the pleasure was all hers. "Matthew, dear," she said, without releasing Susannah's hand, "after you hang up Ms. Bennington's coat, would you go into the kitchen and tell Gertie she can serve the hors d'oeuvres whenever she's ready? Ms. Bennington and I will be in the front parlor—" she drew Susannah forward by the hand she still held, giving it a little pat as she did so "—getting acquainted. We'll wait for you to pour the sherry," she added, the words drifting over her Chanel-clad shoulder as she led her son's guest across the wide foyer and into the front parlor. "Please, sit down," she said, letting go of Susannah's hand to gesture toward a burgundy brocade Victorian settee. She sank gracefully into one of the matching wing chairs arranged opposite it, crossed her ankles, clasped her hands in her lap in approved boarding-school fashion, and smiled at Susannah. "Have you and Matthew known each other long, Ms. Bennington?"

"No, not long," Susannah said, having already resolved to keep to the truth as much as possible. "Just a couple of weeks."

"Oh?" Her glance sharpened. "Then you must be new down at City Hall."

Susannah frowned. "City Hall . . . ?" she began, and then her brow cleared. "Oh, I see what you mean. No, I don't work at City Hall."

"Ah, then you must work at Matthew's campaign office."

"No." Susannah shook her head. "Actually, they probably wouldn't let me in down there. I'm a registered Democrat," she admitted, smiling. "Although I'm planning to vote for Matt, anyway."

"I'm glad to hear that." Millicent returned her smile and came right back to the subject. "So how did you meet, then?"

"Meet?"

"You and Matthew. I don't mean to pry, my dear," she assured her guest. "It's just that Matthew so rarely brings any of his lady friends to visit and, naturally, I'm curious. I hope you don't mind?"

"No. No, of course not," Susannah lied, her glance darting off toward the arched doorway leading to the foyer, wondering what was taking Matt so long in the kitchen. She hadn't thought to ask him what cover story he'd given his mother. "But there's nothing to tell, really. Matt and I aren't . . . That is, I'm not his 'lady friend.' We're just—" she lifted one shoulder in an off-hand shrug "—friends, that's all."

"I see." Millicent leaned forward over the polished marquetry table between them. "And you met how?" she asked, her bright blue eyes full of a mother's questions.

Susannah was abruptly reminded of the way Matt had questioned her in her office; she felt just as compelled to answer now as she had then. It occurred to her that Millicent Ryan might have made a hell of a lawyer if she'd been given the opportunity. "Well, Matt came to my office a couple of weeks ago to, ah . . ."

"Susannah runs a private social-services agency, Mom," Matt said, coming back into the room with a round silver tray of hors d'oeuvres in one hand. "We met when I stopped by her office to check up on a parolee she'd found a job for." He presented the tray to Susannah with a flourish. "Hors d'oeuvre?"

"Yes, thank you." Susannah picked one at random and popped it into her mouth with unladylike haste. She couldn't be expected to talk and chew at the same time.

"Mom?" Matt said, offering the tray to her.

Millicent shook her head. "No, thank you, dear."

"Sherry?" he asked, putting the tray down on the marquetry table.

"Yes, please. There's a brand-new bottle of sherry on the sideboard, waiting to be opened. Pour Ms. Bennington a glass, too," she instructed, watching as he turned to do her bidding. "Here," she said quietly, extending a cocktail napkin toward Susannah. "You can dispose of it in this. There's a brass wastebasket next to the sideboard," she said, looking politely away as Susannah discreetly lifted the small monogrammed paper napkin to her mouth. "I can't stand the ones made with anchovy paste, either," she confided as Susannah crumbled the napkin in her hand. "But I haven't got the heart to tell Gertie to stop making them. She thinks because I'm descended from Swedes I'll eat anything made with fish." Her smile was impish, the expression in her eyes just a bit wistful. "Actually, my husband was the only one who ate the vile things. He loved them."

"Your sherry, Mom."

Millicent lifted her hand for the glass. "Thank you, dear."

"And Susannah," he said, handing it to her as he sat down on the brocade settee beside her.

Susannah took the glass with a murmur of thanks and lifted it to her lips. She almost sighed with pleasure as the bone-dry, straw-colored liquid washed the lingering taste of anchovies off her tongue.

"Excellent sherry, isn't it?" said Millicent, with a twinkling smile.

Susannah smiled back. "Excellent," she agreed and took another small sip before setting the small, footed glass down on the marquetry table. It was time to get down to business. "Matt tells me you're a sponsor of the Junior Symphony," she said pleasantly. "Are they performing tonight at Davies Hall?"

Millicent shook her elegantly coiffed head. "Tonight is a performance in the Summer Pops series," she said, referring to the symphony's summer program of lighter, popular music as opposed to the heavier classics offered during the regular symphony season. "The original Temptations are singing with the symphony tonight. I'm quite looking forward to it."

Susannah smiled. "You're a fan of the Temptations?"

"Oh, yes. I like all kinds of music."

Susannah lifted a teasing auburn eyebrow. "Heavy metal? Rap?"

"Some of it," Matt's mother said serenely. "I think that young black woman—Queen Latifah, I believe her name is—is quite good. She sends a very positive message to young women."

Matt's lifted eyebrow was disbelieving rather than teasing, as Susannah's had been. "Where in the world did you hear Queen Latifah?" he asked, surprised by his mother's revelation.

"Right here in this house," Millicent said. "Gertie's granddaughter listens to her music. She listens to someone called Doggy-something-or-other, too." Matt's mother made a small, well-bred moue of distaste. "I don't like *him* at all."

"You let her listen to that stuff here?" Matt asked, his expression faintly shocked.

Millicent gave him a mild look. "I doubt it's any worse than what you listened to in this house when you were her age." She smiled confidingly at Susannah. "Jimi Hendrix. The Rolling Stones. The Who. Pink something-or-other."

Susannah cut a quick, teasing glance at Matt. "You were a Pink Floyd fan?"

Matt shrugged. "Everybody knows teenagers have no taste," he said in his own defense.

"Well, *I* quite liked most of it," Millicent said. "Although—" she laughed softly "—his father was always shouting at him to turn his stereo down before someone's eardrums were broken. I'm afraid Francis wasn't a fan of rock music."

"And did he turn it down?" Susannah asked, with another teasing glance at her pretend date.

"Yes, he did. Matthew has always been a good boy. A wonderful son." Millicent smiled across the coffee table at Matt. "I don't know what I would have done without him these last two years."

"It must have been very hard for you," Susannah murmured, delicately probing for insight and information about Millicent Larson Ryan. Since Millicent had already mentioned her husband, Susannah felt it would be okay to continue along that track. "Losing your husband after thirty-seven years."

"Oh, my, yes." Millicent sighed pensively. "I was something of a basket case for a good long while after it happened."

"I'm sorry," Susannah said, instantly regretting having pursued the subject. "I shouldn't have brought it up."

"Oh, no, dear, it's quite all right," Millicent assured her. "It took me some time but I've finally come to terms with my—" she smiled lovingly at her son again "—*our* loss," she corrected herself. "It was a tragedy and I'll miss Francis until the day I die, but life does go on. I think we owe it to our loved ones to make the very best of it we can."

THE DOORBELL RANG a few minutes later, announcing the arrival of the rest of Millicent Ryan's guests. Susannah found herself slipping effortlessly back into an old mold, making polite conversation with some of the cream of San Francisco society, while unobtrusively observing Millicent's interaction with her guests in order to learn more about her and trying to be inconspicuous at the same time. But finally, inevitably, one distinguished old dowager recognized her.

"Why, Susannah Bennington, as I live and breath. Goodness, I haven't seen you since . . . well, it must be since Meryl's wedding. How have you been?"

"I'm fine, Mrs. Filbert." Susannah smiled graciously and wondered how soon she could escape. "How are you? And how's Meryl doing these days?"

"She had her second baby three months ago. Another boy. I'm sure she must have sent you an announcement."

"Yes, she did." The birth announcement had been beautifully hand-lettered by a professional calligrapher on thick, handmade paper with a matching envelope. Susannah remembered thinking that the birth announcements had probably cost more than the birth itself. Meryl had always been a show-off, even in elementary school.

"Meryl's so good about those things. So conscientious."

So pretentious.

"Oh, I know she'll be just thrilled to see you." Mrs. Filbert gushed on, reaching out to give Susannah's hands a little squeeze. "She couldn't come to Millicent's little cocktail party tonight—she's one of those dedicated modern mothers who likes to put the children to bed herself." She flapped a heavily beringed hand at Susannah. "I tell her it's a wonder that overpriced British nanny she hired doesn't just die of boredom, she has so little to do."

Susannah's smile became less gracious and more fixed as she remembered that pretentiousness was a Filbert family trait. "You'll have to tell her I said hello, then," she murmured.

"Oh, you can tell her yourself. She and her husband are meeting us later at Davies Hall. And I'm sure she'll want to hear all about whatever it is you're doing now. Are you still with those social-services people?"

"No, not for a while now. I run a—"

"Meryl always said it was so noble of you to work with all those criminals and juvenile delinquents, who I'm sure have no idea how fortunate they are to have you working so tirelessly on their behalf. Why," she huffed theatrically, apparently unaware that Susannah's smile had faded completely, "Meryl told me how ungrateful some of them are. She worked herself nearly ragged, arranging a concert at one of those homeless shelters, just to bring a little culture into their lives, you understand, and hardly any of them even bothered to thank her for her efforts. Can you believe that?"

"Excuse me, Barbara," Millicent Ryan cut in smoothly before Susannah could answer, "but I'm going to have to drag Susannah away. You don't mind, do you? She and Matthew have to leave in a few minutes and I need to have a private word with her before they go."

"Oh, you're not coming to the concert with the rest of us? Meryl will be *so* disappointed."

"Be sure to tell her hello for me," Susannah managed, baring her clenched teeth in a patently false smile. Mrs. Filbert didn't seem to notice the difference. "It was nice seeing you again," she added mendaciously, good manners having been drummed into her at an early age.

"I'm sorry about that," Millicent said as she looped her arm through Susannah's and steered her toward the foyer. "That woman is a hopeless snob and she hasn't got a clue about what goes on in the real world. But she's one of the largest contributors to the symphony fund, not to mention Matthew's political campaign, so . . ." She shrugged eloquently and let it go at that.

"Thanks for rescuing me," Susannah whispered. "I guess you could tell I was about to blow."

"Oh, my dear." Millicent gave a little trill of laughter. "You're very welcome. But it wasn't I who noticed the steam coming out of your ears. It was Matthew. He sent me to get you. Here she is, dear, temper intact," she said to her son as they entered the foyer, "and none the worse for wear."

Millicent stood back, watching consideringly as Matt solicitously helped Susannah on with her coat. Then she stepped forward and took Susannah's shoulders in her hands. "It was lovely to meet you," she said, surprising Susannah with a light kiss on the cheek. "I hope you'll visit again." She turned to her son, presenting her cheek for his goodbye kiss. "Have a nice dinner, you two," she said cheerily, and went back to her other guests.

Susannah waited to comment on that until they were on the other side of the front door. "Dinner?" she said, giving Matt a slanted, sideways look.

Matt shrugged, trying to appear nonchalant. "I had to give her some reason why we weren't going on to the concert with the rest of them."

"Oh." That made sense. "Right." She tugged the lapels of her camel-hair coat closer against the creeping San Francisco fog and followed him down the wide front steps and through the open wrought-iron gate to the sidewalk.

"I was planning on grabbing a quick bite to eat somewhere after I dropped you off at your place." He glanced at her as they crossed the sloping sidewalk to the American-made luxury car parked at the curb. "But if you haven't eaten yet . . . ?"

"Well, no," she said slowly, knowing she shouldn't even be thinking what she was thinking, "I haven't, but . . ."

"I know this great little out-of-the-way place in North Beach," Matt said as he opened the car door for her.

"Italian?"

Matt nodded. "Of course."

"Hmm." Susannah hesitated, as if her mind weren't already made up. "Italian *is* my favorite."

"And you have to eat tonight, anyway."

"True."

"We could discuss what you learned about my mother tonight. What kind of man you think she'd like."

"A business dinner?"

Matt nodded. If she wanted to call it a business dinner, that was fine by him—just as long as they both knew what was really going on. "Sure," he said, "why not?"

"All right," she said, throwing caution and good sense to the wind. She got into the car. "Italian it is, then."

4

THEY HAD TO PARK around the corner from the North Beach restaurant, in a small lot with one light pole and uneven pavement. A short, poorly lit alley ran between the buildings to the street. Matt used the less-than-perfect conditions as the perfect excuse to touch Susannah, cupping her elbow to guide her around a pothole and then, a moment later, sliding his hand to the small of her back, ostensibly to guide her in the direction of the restaurant.

Smooth move, thought Susannah, making no protest when his hand moved from the small of her back to gently ride the curve of her waist. It wasn't as if he could actually feel anything through the heavy fabric of her coat, anyway. And his hand did feel good there. Warm and, well, just…good. His arm behind her back made her feel oddly sheltered, as if he would protect her from any dangers lurking in the shadows.

Not, she assured herself, that she actually needed any protection. Once they were through the alley and out on the sidewalk, the footing was perfectly even and safe. And there were so many people around that it was hard to avoid being jostled by them. The worst that could happen was that she might get her purse snatched.

But she still didn't move away from his touch.

"DO YOU LIKE Chianti?" Matt asked a few minutes later, without even opening the leather-bound wine list the waiter had handed to him.

Susannah barely glanced up from her menu. "Chianti's fine," she said, her mouth already watering at the descriptions of Italian delicacies listed on the menu.

"Two glasses of the house wine," Matt ordered, handing the wine list back to the waiter. "And an order of bruschet—" he broke off and glanced across the table. "Do you object to garlic?"

Susannah raised an eyebrow. "In Italian food?"

Matt smiled, acknowledging her point. "An order of bruschetta to start," he said to the waiter. "Then I'll have the eggplant parmigiana. Susannah?" He waited until she looked up at him again. "Are you ready to order?"

Susannah closed her menu, giving in to temptation without a fight. "Three-cheese lasagna with white sauce," she said, promising herself she'd only eat half of it. She handed her menu to the waiter with a smile of thanks.

"Very good," the waiter said approvingly, as if they had ordered exactly what he would have chosen himself. He took the menus and the wine list and disappeared.

It was very quiet at the small cloth-draped table after the waiter left. Too quiet. Unnervingly quiet. A veritable haven of quiet in the busy little restaurant. They smiled at each other across the candlelit table, suddenly uneasy, oddly hesitant.

Susannah moved her spoon a millimeter closer to her knife and tried desperately to think of something to say.

Matt positioned the saltshaker more precisely on the tablecloth and wondered what had happened to his savoir faire.

They both reached for their water glasses at the same time.

Susannah took a sip of water.

Matt took a sip of water.

They put the glasses down at the same instant and chanced another fleeting glance at each other, another nervous smile.

Susannah looked down and adjusted the napkin in her lap.

Matt reached out and plucked a slender bread stick from the container sitting in the middle of the table. He broke it in half between his long fingers. "Bread stick?" he asked, feeling like a fool. He hadn't been this tongue-tied around a woman since junior high school.

"Yes, thank you," Susannah said gratefully, reaching for it as if he'd offered her a lifeline.

They nibbled in silence for another long few seconds.

"Good bread sticks."

"Yes, they are."

More silence.

"How did you—"

"How is—"

They gazed at each other for a full five seconds, and then, mercifully, burst out laughing at their adolescent silliness. It broke the tension, freeing them from the stilted, unnatural silence.

"You go ahead," Susannah invited graciously.

"Ladies first," Matt insisted gallantly.

"I was only going to ask how your campaign is going."

Matt shrugged. "According to the *Examiner*, I'm ahead in the polls. According to the *Chronicle*, I'm behind. Which means it's way too early to be making any predictions. Especially when you realize that over half the people polled have absolutely no idea who I am in the first place. District judge isn't one of those positions most people know, or care, anything about," he explained with a shrug.

"What does your campaign manager think about your chances?"

"Harry says if I get out there and campaign hard for the next five months, I'm a shoo-in come November. Provided I don't make any really stupid mistakes in the meantime, that is."

"You don't sound as if you agree with him."

"Oh, I agree with him. I think I stand an excellent chance of winning my father's old seat on the bench. I just don't like the idea very much, that's all."

"You don't like the idea of what?" Susannah's expressive eyebrows rose. "Winning your father's old seat?"

Matt gave her a look that said she should know better than that. "Campaigning," he said dryly.

Susannah shook her head. "And you call yourself a politician," she chided playfully.

"I call myself a lawyer," he corrected. "And I can't be a lawyer and campaign the way Harry expects me to at the same time."

"Then why are you running for district judge? You had to know what it would involve before you agreed to it."

"You'd think so, wouldn't you?"

"Are you saying you *didn't* know?"

"Oh, I knew," he admitted. "On some basic level, anyway. I just didn't expect the process to be so . . ." He fell discreetly silent as the waiter returned to set their wine and appetizer on the table. "All-encompassing," he finished when the waiter was out of earshot again.

"All-encompassing how?"

"Campaigning tends to take over your life," Matt said. "And it can easily become a full-time job, if you let it. I can't afford to let it. I've got a court calendar that's backed up from here to last Christmas. The Delaney murder trial is scheduled for August and one of my key witnesses has suddenly changed her mind about what she saw. The conviction in the Mendoza drug case is up for appeal." He shook his head. "Despite what Harry says, I can't be running around to every pancake breakfast and Rotary Club luncheon to shake hands and make speeches. I have more impor—" He broke off suddenly and stared at her across the width of the small table. She was leaning slightly forward, chin balanced on her fist, head tilted, listening raptly to every word he said. "So this is how you get your clients to spill their guts," he said, more than a bit discomforted to realize he'd been spilling his. He wasn't usually so forthcoming. "Very sneaky."

Susannah ignored the teasing comment. "It sounds to me as if you're not completely committed to the campaign," she said, her expression serious and thoughtful. "Are you sure you want to be a judge?"

Matt stared at her for a second, nonplussed. No one had ever asked him that question before, not directly. He hadn't even asked it of himself. "Of course I want to be a judge," he said lightly. "I've wanted it my whole life."

Just not yet.

He hastily pushed the traitorous, unwelcome thought aside and reached for his wineglass. Holding it aloft, he waited until Susannah echoed his gesture and lifted hers, too. "To romance," he said, deliberately changing the subject.

"Romance?" Susannah murmured, disconcerted by the abrupt change of topic.

"My mother's," he clarified, smiling innocently at her over the rim of his glass. His savoir faire, he was happy to note, was firmly back in place. The nerves were gone. And thoughts of whether he did or didn't want to run for district judge were best left for another time. "The one she's going to have as soon as you find her a suitable date."

"Oh. Yes, of course," Susannah agreed. It *was* the reason they were having dinner together. "To romance." She took a small, quick sip of her wine and put it down. "I think you'll be pleased to know that, after meeting her tonight, I think I have the perfect man."

"Oh?" He lifted a thin slice of bruschetta—grilled garlic bread coated with a mixture of chopped tomatoes, onions, garlic, capers and herbs—and placed it on a small plate in front of Susannah before taking one for himself. "Who?"

"I don't think you'd know him. He hasn't been in California long." She picked up her bruschetta between two fingers. "Ever hear of Carlisle Elliott?"

Matt shook his head.

"He's a widower. Sixty-four. Average height. Average weight. Very healthy and active. And quite attractive, too. He looks a little like Cesar Romero, only shorter. Anyway, he moved out here six months ago after selling his nursery business in Iowa." Susannah took a bite of the single slice of bruschetta she'd already determined was all she was going to allow herself, pausing for a moment to savor the sublime mixture of tastes. "He lives over in Sausalito," she said, after she had swallowed. "On a houseboat."

"He lives on a houseboat?" Matt's savoir faire deserted him again for a brief moment as he watched Susannah lick a bit of crushed tomato off the side of her finger with the tip of her little pink tongue.

"Now, don't be a snob, Matt," Susannah advised him, completely misinterpreting the strangled note in his voice. "Your mother certainly isn't. And she's the one who'll be going out with him."

"So your grandmother left you the house and a trust fund. That still doesn't tell me how you got from County Social Services to The Personal Touch," Matt said, handing her an extra fork so she could share his cannoli. Although she'd declined to order a dessert for herself, she'd looked at his as if it were the Holy Grail and the Hope Diamond combined. "From what I know of you so far, I'd have expected you to open a halfway house or a shelter for battered women or something along those lines. Not a dating service."

Susannah looked at him, surprised that he'd pegged her so accurately in such a short time. "I thought about it," she admitted. "I even did some preliminary legwork in that direction. But the area isn't zoned for that kind of establishment. And, to be honest—" she shrugged, still feeling a little guilty for taking the easy way out "—I was tired of all the misery and suffering I saw every day in my job as a social worker. I wanted to do something that would help people make their lives happier, without making myself unhappy in the process." She smiled ruefully and took a minuscule piece of cannoli onto the tip of her fork. "Dottie, my supervisor at County, always said I got too personally involved with my cases."

"No kidding?" he said, amused.

"Yes. Well . . ." She slipped the tiny portion of dessert between her lips, closing her eyes for a second to savor the taste. "Anyway," she said, opening her eyes again, "it seemed to me that running an old-fashioned dating service would be the perfect thing. And it is. I love what I'm doing now. And I'm good at it. I have a very high success rate," she told him. "It's one of the best in the business."

"Yet you're still involved in social work."

"How do you figure that?"

"Judy Sukura," Matt said. "And that other woman you have working for you. The older one who doesn't like men."

"Helen Sanford."

He nodded. "Helen. I'll bet she just didn't answer a want ad for a secretary," he said shrewdly.

"Well, no," Susannah admitted, and helped herself to another tiny bite of his cannoli. "I was introduced to her through a friend who runs a support group for displaced homemakers. You know, women who suddenly find themselves in the workplace with no skills or experience?"

"I know," Matt said, watching as she carefully licked the tines of the fork to get the last bit of whipped cream. "I also know there are organizations to deal with the problem. Programs to teach those women the skills they need before they go out into the workplace."

"Yes, there are programs," Susannah admitted, "but not nearly enough of them." She put her fork down to avoid further temptation. "And Helen actually has plenty of skills, anyway, because she ran her husband's home-based plumbing business for twenty-five years. As so often happens, though, that kind of experience doesn't seem to count in the real world."

"So this friend who runs the support group conned you into hiring Helen to give her some experience."

"I wasn't conned into anything," Susannah objected. "With Judy taking on more hours at school, I needed a full-time assistant and—"

"And Helen was the best person for the job?" he said, his skepticism plain on his face.

"Yes," Susannah lied.

"Uh-huh," he commented, a knowing gleam in his eye. "I'll concede that she might have the technical skills you were looking for, but I seriously doubt her personality is exactly what you had in mind. Here—" he said, lifting his cannoli-laden fork to her mouth when she opened it to object to his characterization of her assistant "—have the last bite."

Susannah either had to open her mouth wider or end up with whipped cream and sweetened ricotta all over her chin. She opened her mouth, accepting the rich dessert will ill-disguised eagerness.

Matt watched her lips part to accept his offering, watched them close over the creamy sweet on his fork, watched her eyelids flutter down as she savored the taste. He withdrew the fork slowly, so that she could get every last bit of the whipped cream, deliberately letting the tines slide against her bottom lip in a sensual caress. "Good?" he murmured huskily.

"Mmm," she sighed ecstatically as the flavors melted on her tongue.

Matt shifted on his chair as his body responded to her unthinking provocation. She was such a contradiction, sitting there across from him: the prim black dress, so striking against her pale, creamy skin, the ladylike pearls, gleaming wantonly at her throat and ears, the sedate chignon, just begging to be released from its pins. Behind the relentlessly refined, implacably genteel exterior she'd presented to him tonight was a warm, passionate, vibrant woman—the same woman who'd melted into his kiss like honey on hot biscuits. "You have no idea how much I want you," he said softly.

Susannah's eyes flew open. "What?" she whispered.

He met her wide-eyed gaze head-on. "You heard me."

Something about his unwavering directness inspired the same unflinching honesty in her. "Yes, I heard you," she said. "And it's crazy. I *know* it's crazy. But I want you, too."

"So," HE SAID as he pulled onto the apron of concrete in front of her narrow garage door. "Are you going to invite me in for coffee?"

Susannah caught her lower lip between her teeth and stared straight ahead. "I shouldn't."

"Probably not," Matt agreed. He stretched his arm out, resting it along the back of the seat, and reached out to twine his finger in the curling tendril of hair that lay against her cheek. "But are you going to?" he asked, tugging lightly to make her look at him.

Susannah turned her head toward him. "It would only be for coffee," she warned him. "I meant what I said about—" she took a quick little breath as he lightly stroked her cheek and down the side of her throat with the back of his finger "—about wanting you. But I haven't decided if I'm going to act on the feeling. I don't think it would be a good idea to rush in when I'm not sure where it will le—"

"When," he said.

"What?"

"You said *if* you decide to act on the feeling. Be as honest as you were in the restaurant, Susannah. It's only a matter of *when*."

"All right, when," she admitted. "I haven't decided *when*." Her gaze was earnest and sweet and serious in the dim light. "But it won't be tonight, Matt. I don't know you well enough, for one thing. And I'm not entirely sure about this...." Her hands fluttered up and then back down into her lap. "This feeling, for an-

other. It kind of snuck up on me when I wasn't expecting it. I have to give this whole situation some serious
thought before I decide what I'm going to do."

"Okay." Matt nodded, manfully hiding his disap-
pointment. "I can understand that. Tonight is out." He
stroked her cheek again, gently, delicately, reveling in
its warmth and softness. "But I'd still like that coffee."

MATT FOUND the interior of Susannah's house to be as
much of a dichotomy as she was. Downstairs, in the
public rooms he'd already seen, the mood and decor
were cozy, elegant and reassuringly conventional. The
colors were soft and soothing, a mix of pale yellows,
soft green and robin's-egg blue. The furnishings were
mostly French and English antiques in light, delicate
woods. The computer terminal on the desk in the reception area had been rendered unobtrusive, half-
hidden behind a large, lacy Boston fern. It didn't take
a genius to realize that everything downstairs had been
deliberately designed to put her customers at ease, to
make them feel as comfortable as if they were part of a
more genteel era, when people first glimpsed their future spouses over tea in great-aunt-somebody's front
parlor instead of at a bar during Happy Hour.

Upstairs, in her personal quarters, it was very different. Oh, it was still delightfully cozy. And undis-
putedly elegant. But nothing about her private space
would ever be called conventional. Matt thought
whimsically that stepping through the heavy wooden
door at the top of the stairs was a little bit like stepping
into a parallel universe; instantly recognizable but,
somehow, just slightly off kilter.

The high ceilings and distinctively detailed crown moldings matched the ones downstairs. The tall, narrow windows were duplicates of those in the front parlor, right down to the fireplace between the two facing the street. The floors were made of the same beautifully polished hardwood. Everything else was delightfully different.

Most of the walls had been knocked out, creating one "great" room out of several smaller ones. Those that were left were painted a deep, rich amethyst, the color defined and intensified by the stark white moldings and woodwork. The windows had been draped and swagged in layers of gauzy white fabric that pooled on the gleaming hardwood floor. The original oak mantel had been removed from the fireplace, replaced with a larger, less ornate one made of pink-veined white marble. The three sofas arranged in a U-shape in front of the fireplace were oversized, overstuffed and low to the ground, designed with the sensual, rounded lines reminiscent of the art-deco period. They were upholstered in deep teal blue and piled high with plump pillows in shades of violet, heliotrope, amethyst, tea-rose pink and deep, dark grape. The only other major piece of furniture in the room was a massive French armoire with pink silk tassels dangling from the door handles. The occasional tables were Art Nouveau reproductions. The wall sconces and lamps were made of frosted glass, shaped like open fans or gracefully drooping lilies, respectively. The fireplace was guarded by a realistically poised and painted pair of seated leopards. One of them wore a wide choker of sparkling rhinestones around its regal neck. The other sported a black satin bow tie and rakishly tilted silk top hat.

"Have a seat," Susannah invited, gesturing toward the sofas. "The coffee will only take a minute." She moved toward the back of the room, quickly, shrugging out of her camel-hair coat as she went. She tossed it over the padded seat of one of the six high-backed stools surrounding the freestanding, white marble counter that served as her dining table and separated her kitchen area from the rest of the room. "I can make espresso or cappuccino, if you'd rather," she said from behind the counter. "I have a machine."

"Espresso sounds good." Matt followed her into the kitchen, drawn to her like metal filings to a magnet. He came up behind her as she reached out to open the refrigerator, coming close enough to lean down and sniff the back of her neck. "That's not the same perfume you were wearing the other day."

Susannah gave a muffled shriek and whirled around, nearly bumping into him in the process. The refrigerator door banged shut. "What?"

He took the bottle of springwater from her and put it down on the counter next to the espresso machine. "Your perfume. It's not the same one you were wearing the other day."

"No, it isn't." She edged away from him, trying to be casual about it, and began filling the water receptacle on the machine. "It was a gift."

"This or the other?"

"This."

"I'd get rid of it," he advised, jealous of whoever had given it to her. "It isn't you."

"Oh?" she said, turning her head to look at him. He was much too close. She turned her gaze back to the espresso machine.

"It's much too flowery and sweet," he said in answer to her hasty look. "I like the other better."

"I'll try to remember that." She flipped the lid down on the water receptacle and sidled down the counter, reaching up to open the cupboard where she keep the coffee.

Matt's hand closed over hers on the white ceramic knob, as if he had inadvertently raised his hand at the same moment. "Can I help?" he asked innocently.

Susannah swallowed nervously. She slipped her hand from under his and backed away a step, coming smack up against the refrigerator door. "Why don't you go and put on some music?" she suggested. "My audio system is in the armoire." She lifted a hand, gesturing toward the living area.

Matt caught it in his. "Are you afraid of me, Susannah?"

"No, of course not."

"Nervous, then?"

"No," she lied.

He rubbed his thumb over the back of her hand, slowly, as if testing its softness—and her veracity.

"Okay, maybe." She gave a noncommittal little shrug, trying to be blasé about the warm tingles of sensation zinging up her arm. "A little," she admitted reluctantly, then gave him a stern look. "But only because you're crowding me."

Matt laughed softly. Triumphantly. He took a half a step back. "There's no need to be nervous," he assured her, and lifted her hand to his mouth. "Not tonight, anyway," he added, and pressed a warm kiss into her palm.

It took all of Susannah's considerable willpower to keep from curling her hand into the heat of his kiss.

His blue eyes gleamed wickedly, as if he knew just how much self-control it was costing her to appear unmoved. "Tonight, I'm on my best behavior."

Susannah couldn't help but smile at that. "And I'm Mother Teresa," she said dryly. She pulled her hand out of his grasp. "Go put on some music and let me make the espresso."

He hesitated a moment, just long enough for her to wonder if he was going to be difficult. And then he sighed, theatrically, like a small boy who had been denied a longed-for treat, and went to do as she'd bid him. Susannah was still smiling as she measured coffee into the stainless-steel filter. She'd often heard that good trial lawyers were part actor. Now she believed it.

"What would you like to hear?" Matt asked a few moments later. "Rod Stewart, *Unplugged?* Frank Sinatra, *The Columbia Years?* Or Willie Nelson's *Greatest Hits?*"

Susannah lifted two delicate demitasse cups down from the cupboard. She dropped a sugar cube into each one. "You choose," she said and pressed the start button on the espresso machine. It rumbled and thumped and hissed noisily, finally spewing forth a stream of thick rich coffee into the waiting cups. When the cups were full and she finally turned the machine off, her ears were filled with the sound of Ol' Blue Eyes crooning love songs from the Big Band era. *Great.* "Lemon peel?"

she asked, raising her voice to be heard above the music.

"Sounds good," Matt said.

Susannah took that to be a reference to the lemon peel and not the music swirling through the room. She gave the tiny piece of lemon a deft twist and dropped it into his cup. Placing it on a tray next to her own, she took a quick breath, picked up the tray and sailed into the living area with as much aplomb as she could muster.

"Here, let me help you with that," Matt said, standing up to take the tray from her as she rounded the corner of the sofa.

Some of her aplomb abruptly faded away. While she'd been busy preparing the espresso, he'd been busy making himself right at home. He'd switched on the gas fireplace; firelight flickered cheerily off the marble mantel and struck flashing shards of light off the leopard's rhinestone choker. He'd found the brandy; two oversize snifters sat side by side on the pale pink lacquered surface of her coffee table, two fingers of amber liquid in each. He'd located the dimmer switch that controlled the frosted sconces; they glowed palely against the amethyst walls.

He'd also found the time to take off his suit coat and burgundy-and-blue paisley tie, leaving her to stare at a broad chest and shoulders that looked at least a yard wide under the soft white cotton of his custom-made shirt. The hands that reached out for her tray were strong and tanned, bared to the white shirtsleeves rolled halfway up his forearms.

Do men do that on purpose? she wondered pee-
vishly. *Do they all know what the sight of a pair of
strong, hair-dusted forearms does to a woman's resolve? I'll bet he opened those top two buttons on his
shirt on purpose, too,* she decided, *just to show off that
tempting wedge of chest hair.*

"I'm going to punch the next man who dares accuse
women of using their sex appeal to get what they want,"
she muttered as Matt put the tray on the coffee table and
sat down.

He lifted an eyebrow. "Beg pardon?" he said, glancing up at her from the sofa. Somehow, just sitting there
like that, looking up at her, he managed to appear innocently adorable and dangerously, irresistibly sexy at
the same time.

Susannah decided that she absolutely had to assert
herself before things got out of hand. Or more out of
hand than they already were. What on earth had she
been thinking of, anyway, to let him come in for coffee?

"I meant what I said about nothing happening between us tonight," she said firmly, letting her gaze
sweep over the cozy little scene he had set. "I'm not
about to let myself be seduced." *No matter how sexy
and adorable and irresistible you are.*

"And I meant what I said about knowing nothing was
going to happen tonight," Matt said, pretending af-
front that she would doubt him. "I have no intention
of seducing you." He broke eye contact, deliberately
letting his gaze make the same sweep hers had before
bringing it back to her again. "Although I did kind of
hope we might indulge in some heavy necking," he said,

laughing out loud when her mouth fell open. "Relax, Susannah." He reached out and grabbed her hand. "I promise I won't do anything you don't want me to do."

Oh, that's a comfort, she thought, as she bounced down on the cushy sofa beside him.

He picked up one of the cups of espresso on the tray and handed it to her. She took it with an automatic murmur of thanks, eyeing him warily despite his promise.

His lips turned up in a wicked grin. "I also promise I won't make love to you tonight, even if you beg me."

SHE ALMOST BEGGED HIM.

They had finished the espresso and were sipping on the brandy when he leaned over and kissed her. It started out as a gentle kiss, meant to be teasing and playful. But they both caught fire the instant their lips touched and the kiss went from playful to heated in a heartbeat.

Matt put his free hand on the back of her head to bring her closer, to taste her more deeply, to hold her mouth pressed to his as he experimented with the limited pressures and angles possible to them as they sat there on the sofa, knowing they could go no further while they both held brandy snifters. It went on for long, endless, frustrating minutes. Hot, sweet kisses that made him ache like a teenager in the back seat of his father's car, until, finally, he could take no more and raised his head with a ragged sigh.

Susannah stared up at him, her soft brown eyes liquid and warm with wanting, her lips wet and shiny from his. "More," she murmured, as heedless and greedy as a child in a candy store. "Kiss me again, Matt."

It was the way she said his name, all soft and breathy and aching with need, that cracked his resolve. He pulled just far enough away from her to take the brandy snifters and put them on the coffee table. And then he cupped his big hands on either side of her head, cradling it, tilting it back, and took her mouth with his. His lips plucked at hers, sliding over them, wetting and warming them, teasing them, until, helplessly, she opened her mouth as wide as he wanted and invited him in. He took unhurried, undisputed possession. His tongue plunged between her lips, a welcome invader, thoroughly plundering her sweetness, asking to be plundered in return. Susannah obliged him eagerly and they engaged in a heated duel, sharing the dark flavor of espresso, the tang of lemon, the heady taste of brandy warmed by passion's intemperate flames.

They nibbled and nipped, licked and sucked, changing angles and pressures, pulling apart to taste each other's cheeks and chins, ears and eyelids and the soft underside of a jaw, then coming together again in a kiss deeper than the one before.

His hands tangled in her wayward curls, freeing them to fall in glorious disarray over her shoulders. Her fingers threaded through his silky blond hair, holding him to her when he pressed his lips to her throat in a hot, open-mouthed kiss.

"This is madness," she whispered raggedly, pulling him closer.

"Insanity," he agreed with a low growl as he lifted his hands to her nape, seeking the tab of the long zipper that ran down the back of her dress.

She bowed her head against his wide chest and reached up with one hand, brushing her hair aside to make it easier to find. Neither one of them gave a thought to her misgivings or his promise as he slid the tab down to her waist. He moved his hands back up the open V and grasped the loosened bodice of the dress. She straightened as he drew it forward, allowing him to bare her throat and shoulders and the soft swell of her breasts, barely contained in a purple satin demi-bra trimmed with black lace. The straps were halfway down her arms, caught by his fingers as he pulled the bodice of her dress down.

Matt sucked in his breath at her delicate beauty. He leaned down and, very softly, pressed a kiss into the top of her cleavage.

Susannah whimpered. "Absolute madness," she moaned.

The words sobered him.

If he pulled the dress the rest of the way down, if he bared her breasts, there would be no stopping him. Not that she would ask him to stop. Not now. Not with her heart pounding and her body trembling, and passion wreaking havoc on her better judgment. She wouldn't even remember the promise he'd made her until later, when the passion had cooled and she'd had time to consider what she'd done in the searing heat of the moment. He told himself that Susannah was a fair woman, an honest woman, and she wouldn't blame him for what they'd both done.

But she might regret it.

And, damn it, he'd promised.

Matt closed his eyes and his hands clenched on the fabric of her dress, hard, as he fought not to pull it the rest of the way down.

"Matt?" she said uncertainly, her voice trembling almost as much as her body.

He shook his head. "Give me a minute," he rasped. "Just one minute." He took a deep breath and pulled the dress back into place on her shoulders. It was the hardest thing he'd ever done but he made good on his promise.

He just hoped she appreciated it.

She took a deep steadying breath, and then another, struggling to bring her rampaging emotions under control. She wanted to scream and beg, to demand that he finish what they had started. She eased herself away from him, instead. "Thank you," she whispered.

He was just pulling up the zipper on her dress when they heard the downstairs door creak open.

"Are you expecting visitors?"

Susannah frowned. "No, I—"

Heavy footsteps sounded on the stairs. "Suse?" a voice called softly. "You awake up there?"

Susannah's hands flew to her hair. "Oh, goodness, it's Heather."

"Heather?"

"Heather Lloyd. She's staying with me for a while. In the efficiency apartment downstairs."

A light knock reverberated through the room. "Suse?"

Susannah jumped up from the sofa. "Yes, I'm up," she called. "You can come in."

The door opened to reveal a slender teenager dressed in the height of grunge street fashion: torn jeans, baggy sweater hanging down from beneath a worn and studded leather jacket, heavy, black motorcycle boots and short blond hair that looked as if she'd styled it herself with pinking shears. She stood in the doorway for a moment, taking in the scene. "Oh, jeez, Suse. I didn't know you had company." She started to back out the door. "I'll go."

"No, it's all right," Susannah said brightly. "Matt was just leaving." She scooped his jacket and tie off the sofa as she spoke and handed them to him without looking at him, trying to pretend her cheeks weren't blazing red. "Weren't you, Matt?"

"Looks like it," Matt said, standing up to slip into his jacket. He folded the tie and put it in his pocket, then reached out and caught Susannah's chin in his hand, turning her face up to his. "We'll finish this later," he said in a low voice, his eyes intense and predatory as they stared down into hers. "And that's another promise you can count on."

Heather stepped back as he approached the door, watching him warily out of shadowed green eyes. "I don't suppose you want me to, like, call you a taxi or something?" she said hopefully.

Matt paused to look down at her. "No, thanks," he said lightly, realizing she wasn't more than sixteen, if that. What had a kid her age been doing out so late? "My car's parked right outside."

Heather grimaced and hunched her shoulders in protective reflex action. "It wouldn't happen to a navy-blue Lincoln Continental, would it?"

"Yes." Matt nodded slowly, sensing he was about to hear something he wouldn't like. "Why?"

The girl lifted her chin defiantly, causing the multiple earrings dangling from each of her delicate earlobes to sway against one another. "I, like, put an illegal-parking sticker on your windshield," she said, her posture daring him to do something about it.

5

"YOUR JUVENILE delinquent owes me fifteen dollars," Matt informed Susannah over the telephone the next afternoon. Actually, it had cost him a good bit more than that since the You Are Parked Here Illegally sticker she'd slapped on his windshield had had to be thoroughly saturated with a special solvent before the carwash attendant could scrape it off. He'd decided to give her a discount for good intentions—apparently Susannah had been having problems with people parking in her driveway and blocking her in—and for showing a modicum of good sense. At least she hadn't stuck the damn thing on the driver's side and blocked his view. Besides, if he charged her any more than fifteen dollars, Susannah would probably end up paying for it. And it wasn't Susannah who needed to learn a lesson.

"Heather's really sorry about what she did to your car," she assured him.

Matt snorted in disbelief. The girl had been anything but apologetic last night. She'd acted as if the whole thing was his fault for having parked in Susannah's driveway in the first place.

"No, really," Susannah said. "She is. And I know she won't do it again. To anyone. Not after that lecture you gave her."

Matt smiled in grim satisfaction. The grubby little vandal had gone white when he'd pointed out that some gun-wielding hothead might take exception to having his property defaced and take his displeasure out on the house or its inhabitants. He could only hope he'd given her something to think about the next time she was tempted to try some stupid stunt.

"I found a dozen or so of those illegal parking stickers in the trash can by my desk this morning," Susannah said, knowing the silent act of contrition was as close as Heather would get to apologizing. In the world Heather had run away from, admitting fault meant admitting weakness and admitting weakness got you slapped down—or worse. Susannah didn't blame the girl one little bit for her lack of trust and openness.

"Have you arranged that date for my mother yet?" Matt asked, suddenly tired of the subject of Heather Lloyd. He dealt with people like her all day—troubled, in trouble and just plain Trouble.

"I've talked to Mr. Elliott," Susannah said. "Even after I explained your excessive need for subterfuge—" she couldn't resist the gentle dig "—he was still very interested in meeting her. He said she sounds like a, and I quote, lovely, refined gentlewoman, unquote. I told him I'd check with you and get back to him about the date and time."

"How about this Saturday night at seven-thirty?"

"Saturday night?"

"The campaign's hosting a fund-raiser at the Mark Hopkins. I have to make a speech and shake a few hands but it shouldn't be too bad. And the kitchens at the Mark are excellent," he said enticingly. "So you know the food will be good."

"Well, I'll check with Mr. Elliott." She doodled a question mark on her yellow pad. "Will he need a tuxedo or would a business suit be okay?"

"Tuxedo," Matt said. "And if he doesn't have one, tell him I'll spring for the rental as part of the deal."

"How about tickets?"

"Both you and Elliott will come as my guests, naturally."

"Me?" Susannah's heart suddenly started fluttering in her chest. She tried to calm it with flippancy. "I don't recall anything about my appearance at some stuffy political fund-raiser being part of the deal."

"New deal," Matt said. "I need you there to introduce Elliott to my mother."

"You didn't need me to introduce her to the last three candidates."

"And looked what happened."

Susannah thought about that for all of two seconds. "All right, I'll call him right now and get back to you."

She tried to tell herself her eagerness had nothing to do with Matt—and failed miserably. Her eagerness had everything to do with Matt; she'd never in her life actually *wanted* to go to a political fund-raiser.

"I'm due in court in a few minutes but you can leave a message on my voice mail or on the machine at the condo." He gave her the number. "Got that?"

"Mmm-hmm," she said and drew a heart around his home number.

"Good. And, Susannah?"

"Yes?" A ring of hearts began to take shape around his name.

"Even if Elliott can't make it on Saturday, I still want you to go with me." Matt's voice lowered suggestively. "We have unfinished business to take care of."

Susannah put her pencil down. "I hardly think a campaign fund-raiser is the place to take care of it," she said tartly, shocked at the way her heart had begun to thump against her chest.

"Afterward," he promised.

"IF MR. ELLIOTT CALLS back while I'm upstairs, give me a holler, would you, please?" Susannah said as she came hurrying out of her office half an hour later. "I have to check on something." Like whether she had anything decent to wear to a black-tie dinner in the Peacock Court at the Mark Hopkins.

"One sec, Suse," Heather said, putting her hand over the mouthpiece. "I'm, like, on the phone."

Susannah stopped in her tracks and actually focused on who was sitting at the receptionist's desk. Heather never came into the front office during business hours; all parties concerned had decided she'd scare the clients. And what was she doing answering the phone? Her telephone skills were practically nonexistent.

"Yeah," Heather was saying into the receiver. "I'm, like, glad you're happy with the arrangement." She turned slightly away from Susannah as she spoke, lifting one shoulder as if to shield the conversation from her. "Yeah, I'll see you later. I gotta go now. 'Bye."

"Who was that?" Susannah asked when Heather had cradled the receiver. She tried to make her voice casual and undemanding, knowing how touchy teenagers were about their privacy.

"Nobody important." Heather shrugged. "Just a friend."

Susannah nodded and let the subject drop. If Heather didn't want to confide in her, then she didn't. "How come you're here answering the phones?"

"Helen went over to The Tea Cozy to, like, see what was taking Judy so long to, like, you know, check out the food 'n' stuff for your tea party. They'll be back in a coupl'a minutes."

"That still doesn't tell me what you're doing in the office." Susannah gave her a searching look. "Why aren't you in school?" Part of the agreement that allowed the girl to live in Susannah's house included regular attendance at school. "Are you cutting classes?"

"I'm on my lunch hour." Heather hunched her shoulders and shifted into offense. "I just, like, thought I'd come over and find out if the guy you were doin' the nasty with on the couch last night told you what the damages are yet, you know?"

Susannah decided the only dignified thing to do was ignore the reference to last night's activities. "Fifteen dollars."

Heather shrugged, as if it didn't make any difference to her one way or another. She dug into the pocket of her jeans, drawing out a handful of crumpled bills, and peeled off a ten and five ones. The remaining bills totaled less than six dollars, all she'd have until the weekend, when she could sell more of her jewelry creations to the tourists at Fisherman's Wharf. "Give it to him for me, will ya?"

Susannah waved the money away. "Give it to him yourself," she said. "He'll be coming here to pick me up Saturday night."

"Aw, come on, Suse. Saturday night? I'm gonna be, like, you know, busy on Saturday night."

"Come on, yourself," Susannah retorted. "Part of taking responsibility for your life is owning up to your mistakes and making amends in person."

"Couldn't I just, like, mail it to him, instead?"

"It's up to you," Susannah said, her tone aptly conveying how disappointed she'd be if Heather chose that method of dealing with the problem. "It's the coward's way out, though."

Heather frowned. "Okay, Saturday night," she groused, stuffing the money back into the pocket of her grubby jeans. "What time?"

"Between seven and seven-thirty."

Heather nodded. "Okay, I'll make sure to be here. Later." She lifted her hand in a gesture of farewell and headed for the front door.

"Wait."

Heather paused, looking back over her shoulder with a put-upon sigh, half expecting to be called down for something else. "I gotta get back to school."

"Did you eat lunch? Would you like me to make you a sandwich to take with you?"

Heather's smile was unexpectedly sweet. "No thanks, Suse," she said, obviously touched. "I grabbed a Big Mac on the way over, you know?"

SUSANNAH DECIDED that the best course of action was just to be herself. Oh, she could run out and buy something long and formal and boring for this fund-raiser, and Matt would probably love it. After all, he'd seemed pretty taken with the prissy little nun's habit she'd worn last night. But it wouldn't be *her*. And if this relationship—or *whatever* it was that was happening between them—was going to develop into anything at all, it had to be based on total honesty.

And a long, formal boring evening gown from some tony Union Square department store wasn't honest. The 1920s rose-chiffon flapper dress she'd bought herself for her birthday last February was.

She took it out of the closet and unzipped the cloth garment bag she'd stored it in to protect the fragile material. Shaking it out lightly, she reached up and snagged the hook of the padded hanger on the bare brass canopy frame over her bed. The fresh ocean-scented breeze coming in through the open window fluttered the airy layers of the chiffon handkerchief hem, making the dress billow and sway as if it were dancing by itself. Sunlight sparkled on the long, intricately beaded bodice, making it glimmer and shine. It was a perfect dress. *The* perfect dress. If Matthew Ryan didn't fall flat on his face when he saw her in this dress, then he wasn't the man for her.

Smiling to herself, she turned from the bed to the window, intending to close it a bit so that a sudden gust wouldn't blow the delicate dress from its hanger. She paused with her hands on the window sash, her gaze captured by the scene playing itself out on the street below her.

Eddie Devine was standing across the street in front of The Tea Cozy. He had his hands wrapped around Judy's upper arms, holding her captive, talking earnestly, rapidly, emphatically. Judy stood with her head turned down and away as she listened, her whole body straining away from his touch.

Susannah felt the anger boil up. He'd had his one chance, and one was all he was going to get. She wasn't going to stand around while he manhandled Judy a second time.

Slamming the window down, Susannah ran out of the bedroom, through the great room of her upstairs apartment and down the carpeted staircase. She flew into the reception area just as Judy came rushing in from outside.

"Judy, are you all right?" she asked, reaching out to steady the younger woman and help her to a chair. "Are you hurt?"

"I'm all right," Judy said, shrugging away from the helping hands as she sank into the desk chair. "It was nothing."

"Nothing! I saw him grab you." Susannah reached out again, hesitantly, her fingertips hovering over the angry red marks on the soft skin of Judy's upper arms. "You're going to have bruises."

Judy barely glanced down at them. "I'm all right, Susannah. Really," she said, looking up at her employer with eyes too old and experienced to belong to a woman who was barely twenty-one. "He didn't do anything he hasn't done worse before. I'm fine. They're just bruises." She waved away Susannah's concern with a weary gesture. "It's nothing."

"It's not nothing," Susannah insisted. "It's assault. I think you should call the police and file a complaint."

"*No!*" Judy almost came up out of her chair at the suggestion. "No," she said, more calmly. "I don't want the police. I don't need them. It's nothing, really. Eddie was just . . . being Eddie. Just talking big, you know? Trying to scare me into coming back to work for him."

"If you don't do something about it now, he might do something worse next time."

"No." Judy shook her head. "I told him I wouldn't do it. That no matter what he did, he couldn't make me do it. He knows I mean it."

"Well, I sent him on his way," Helen said with satisfaction as she bustled into the office. She hurried over to Judy. "Are you all right, dear? Did he hurt you?"

In an uncharacteristic gesture, Judy reached up and squeezed the hand that reached out to pat her shoulder. "Thanks, Helen," she said softly, and quickly let the hand go.

Susannah looked back and forth between the two women. "Just what exactly went on out there?" she asked.

"Eddie was waiting for me when I came out of The Tea Cozy," Judy said wearily. "Helen was still inside, talking to Jason about the food for the party." Jason was one of the two owners of The Tea Cozy. "Anyway, Eddie said he wanted to talk to me about—" she shrugged uneasily and looked away "—about a new scam or something. I don't know, exactly. When I told him I wasn't interested, he started to get a little rough. That's when Helen came out of the Cozy. She hollered my

name and Eddie let me go. I ran in here. After that—"
She shrugged.

Susannah looked at Helen, silently asking what had
happened after that.

"I gave that lowlife scum a piece of my mind, that's
what happened after that," Helen said. "And you were
right, Susannah, he isn't nearly as tough as he thinks
he is. He changed his tune real fast when I threatened
to mess up his pretty moussed hairdo with my lead
pipe." She pulled the item partway out of her volumi-
nous shoulder bag to show them. "It put the fear of God
into him, I can tell you. He won't be back here bothering Judy again. Not if he knows what's good for him."

"Oh, my goodness." Susannah could feel a little
bubble of laughter working its way up out of her chest
as her mind conjured up a picture of grandmotherly
Helen chasing slick Eddie Devine down the street with
a lead pipe in her hand. "Oh, Helen," she said in a
strangled voice. Despite all she could do, the laughter
spilled over. "I'm sorry," she said. "I know it isn't funny.
But the thought of you—" she choked back a whoop of
laughter "—chasing Eddie down the street...."

"Waving that lead pipe over your head," Judy added,
before breaking into laughter herself.

Helen looked back and forth between her two
laughing co-workers, as if slightly insulted. And then
she smiled. "It would look kind of funny, wouldn't it?"

"OKAY, WE'VE GOT the watercress sandwiches, the cu-
cumber sandwiches, the scones, the shortbread cook-
ies, the tea cakes...." Susannah snatched up one of the
tiny frosted confections and popped it into her mouth.

"The tea and coffee are on the sideboard. Helen, where are the lemon wedges?" she asked, reaching out to reposition the silver sugar bowl to a more attractive angle. "There aren't any lemon wedges."

"Right here," Helen said, hurrying over to place the small glass bowl of sliced fruit on the sideboard.

"Lemon wedges," Susannah said, continuing with her visual inventory, "sugar, milk, cream, cocktail napkins. And fresh lemonade. We're ready for blast-off," she announced, just as the first party guests entered through the front door of The Personal Touch.

In less than a half an hour the reception area and front parlor were crowded with those Personal Touch clients who'd been invited to attend one of Susannah's get-acquainted teas. Although invitations weren't limited to the senior citizens on her client list, the tea parties usually ended up heavily weighted in that direction. Unlike a lot of other dating services in the city, a large part of her clientele was in the fifty-five-and-over age group. She'd found that many of them felt more comfortable meeting new people in an informal setting, alleviating the nerve-racking pressure of a one-on-one encounter. Her late-afternoon teas had proven so popular, she was thinking of adding a dressier evening party to the mix, maybe opening up the doors between the front and back parlors and rolling up the rugs for ballroom dancing.

She filed the thought away for the moment, setting herself the welcome task of mingling with her guests, making sure that those with the most likely chance of hitting it off as a couple met each other.

Three hours later, footsore, talked out and stuffed to the eyebrows with frosted tea cakes, Susannah shut off the lights and went upstairs to figure out what accessories she was going to wear with her flapper dress—and wondering if she had time to fit in a trip to the shoe department at Neiman Marcus before Saturday rolled around.

"You're early," Heather said as she opened the front door at six forty-five the following Saturday evening. "Suse wasn't, like, expecting you for another fifteen minutes, you know?" She gave him a sly knowing grin, calculated to get under his skin. "Guess you, like, couldn't wait to get your hands on her, huh?"

"It's nice to see you, too, Ms. Lloyd," Matt said with exaggerated politeness, ignoring the deliberate provocation of her words. One encounter was all it had taken for him to realize that that's what would bug her the most.

Everything about her was calculated with an eye toward its shock value, from the shaggy hacked-off hair to the storm-trooper boots to the collection of silver pentagrams and crosses hanging from the multiple holes in her ears. She was wearing a cropped cotton sweater tonight, in a drab olive green that did nothing for her delicate complexion, and a pair of cutoff denim shorts that looked as if they'd been rescued from the rag bin. The sweater appeared to be at least two sizes too big; the shorts were a size too small. "Is Susannah upstairs?"

"Uh-huh." Heather let the door swing closed behind him with a careless bang. "She said to, like, bring you up and give you a glass of champagne." She turned and trooped up the stairs ahead of him, her heavy black motorcycle boots clumping loudly on each tread, her slim hips swaying from side to side like a pendulum gone haywire.

It was like watching a cross between Marilyn Monroe in a scene from *Some Like It Hot* and Frankenstein's poor monster stumbling blindly around in the woods. Matt studied the movement as he climbed the stairs behind her, trying to figure out if she was doing it on purpose or if it was her natural walk.

Heather glanced over her shoulder. "See anything you like?" she said with a provocative pout. No doubt perfected, he thought, after hours spent studying Drew Barrymore's *Guess?* ads.

"Give it ten or fifteen years, kid," he said dryly, his expression bored and deliberately patronizing. "By then you might have enough experience to make it interesting."

Amazingly, the pout shifted into a smile before she mastered her expression and turned away. "Hey, Suse," she hollered as they entered the upstairs apartment. "The ambulance chaser is here." She shot him another sly look to see how he reacted to the slur on his profession, but there was no real malice in her eyes this time.

Matt felt as if he'd passed some test he hadn't even known he'd taken.

"You, like, want some champagne?" Heather asked, reaching for the bottle on the counter as she spoke.

Matt crooked his fingers at her in a beckoning motion. "Give it to me," he said, "I'll open it."

"I can—"

He leaned across the counter and took it out of her hand. "It's not that I don't trust you...." He let his voice trail off.

Heather grinned and held out her hand, palm up, for the foil wrapping.

He was just pouring champagne into a fluted glass when Susannah walked out of the bedroom. Matt sucked in his breath and stared.

Her hair was down, the way it had been the first time he'd seen her. Springy corkscrew curls framed the pale oval of her face and cascaded over her shoulders, a rich, lustrous mahogany red against the silky creaminess of her bared skin. Her dress was soft and pink and floaty, with thin straps made of sparkly beads and a U-shaped neckline that dipped just low enough to hint at the beginning swell of her breasts. The whole thing seemed to shimmer, catching and reflecting the light with her slightest breath.

Susannah hesitated just outside her bedroom door, her smile fixed and uncertain, waiting for Matt to react in a way she could interpret. Was his stunned silence good or bad? Was he bowled over with admiration for her elegant and sophisticated taste? Or wondering if she was really going to out in public dressed like a Las Vegas chorus girl?

"Tell her she looks nice," Heather hissed, just as Matt felt ice-cold champagne trickle over his fingers and onto the floor. He jerked the champagne bottle upright, setting it, and the overflowing flute, down on the marble counter with a sharp click.

"You look incredible, Susannah." He shook his head slightly, as if to clear it. "Absolutely stunning."

Susannah's smiled bloomed with relief and she let out the breath she didn't even know she'd been holding. Her self-confidence miraculously restored by his obvious admiration, she stepped out of the doorway and walked across the room toward him, slowly, never once taking her eyes from his. The heels of her new evening shoes clicked against the hardwood floor. The uneven hand-kerchief hem of her dress flirted with her slender calves, concealing and revealing them with every step. The hip-length beaded bodice sparkled around her slim torso, making her look as if she were surrounded by stardust.

She stopped in front of Matt, close enough for him to smell the exotic oriental fragrance she'd used in her bath, and reached up to straighten his perfectly straight black satin bow tie.

"So do you," she said softly. "Look incredible, I mean."

And he did. Most men looked a little uncomfortable in black tie, as if they weren't quite sure everything was on right. Matt looked born to it, as elegant and at ease as a royal Scandinavian prince. Tall, blond, broad-shouldered and almost icily remote. Until he smiled and reached up to take her hands in his. He lifted them to his lips, one at a time, and the look in his eyes as he pressed his mouth to each of her sensitive palms in turn wasn't remote at all. It burned hot enough to melt gla-ciers—or a woman's foolish heart.

Heather's low whistle intruded into the taut silence. "It's, like, wow, Cinderella and frigging Prince Charming," she said admiringly.

Susannah laughed softly, shakily, and slipped her hands out of Matt's in an effort to regain the equilibrium he'd stolen with just a smile and a heated look. Matt let her slide her fingers from his without protest, his look telling her—*promising* her—that she wouldn't get away so easily next time . . . that if it hadn't been for Heather standing there watching them and the people waiting for them at the hotel, she wouldn't have gotten away this time.

Susannah shivered with a combination of instinctive feminine fear and delicious anticipation and turned away from the look in his eyes. "Do we have time for a glass of champagne before we go?" she asked, already reaching out for one of the delicate fluted glasses on the marble counter. She turned her head, glancing over her shoulder when he didn't answer immediately. "Matt?"

Matt answered with a strangled syllable that sounded suspiciously like a curse.

Heather giggled.

Susannah raised a delicate eyebrow.

"Good God, woman," Matt demanded, "do you want to start a riot?"

Susannah's eyebrow rose higher. "Excuse me?" she said, although she knew exactly what he meant.

The back of her dress dipped considerably lower than the front, coming to a V just above her waistline. Three strands of crystal beads draped across her spine, filling in the opening and holding the dress in place.

Matt made another inarticulate noise and gestured at the back of her dress.

Susannah shrugged, making the beaded strands shimmy over her skin, and turned back to the counter. She nonchalantly reached for the champagne, secretly pleased to be getting some of her own back. He'd disconcerted her with a smile and a heated look; she'd evened the score with a little discreetly bared flesh. "Do you think it's too much?" she asked innocently, and winked at Heather.

"I think it's—" *the sexiest thing I've ever seen"*—too damned little," he groused. "You're going to catch pneumonia if you go outside in that thing."

"My evening wrap is very warm." She turned back to face him. "Champagne?" she said, and held his glass toward him with a bright smile of feminine challenge.

Matt looked at her for a long second, consideringly, fighting the twin urges to wring her neck and kiss her senseless at the same time. He decided that neither one was a viable option at the moment. He reached out and took the glass from her, draining half of it with one gulp. "We'd better get going if we don't want to be late," he said, handing the glass back to her.

Susannah took it and set it on the counter. She looked at the teenager who stood silently, watching them. "Heather? Don't you have something you want to say to Matt before we leave?"

Heather twisted her hands in the hem of her sweater, pulling it all out of shape, and shrugged noncommittally.

Susannah gave her a sharp look, tilted her head toward Matt, and then turned to get her wrap, leaving the two of them to talk privately.

"Suse thinks I should, like—" she looked at the floor, her mouth screwed up in a rueful grimace "—apologize, you know?"

"And what do you think?"

She shrugged again.

Matt waited.

Heather sighed and dug into the pocket of her shorts. "Here." She handed him a wad of bills. "What I owe you." The next words she uttered could have been *I'm sorry* but they were mumbled so low Matt couldn't be sure.

He smoothed the bills out, wondering if he should make her say it again, and then decided to let her off the hook. This time. "Thanks." He folded the bank notes neatly in half and slipped them into his pocket.

"Everything okay here?" Susannah asked as she came back with her wrap over her arm.

Heather looked at Matt.

He nodded.

"Did she ask your advice about her legal problem?"

"*Suse!*"

"What legal problem?" Matt asked warily. There was no end of legal trouble a teenager could get into these days, especially one with an attitude and no discernible parental influence.

"I've got it covered," Heather said, shooting a fulminating look at Susannah. "Legal Aid assigned me a lawyer yesterday afternoon. I forgot to tell you, is all."

"A lawyer?" Susannah huffed delicately. "Some first-year law student, right?"

"Second year," Heather said. "And all he has to do is, like, file some stupid papers is all. It's no big deal."

"What legal problem?" Matt demanded in a quiet tone that nevertheless had both females turning their heads to look at him.

"I'm petitioning the court to be declared an emancipated minor," Heather told him.

"That involves more than just filing a few papers," he said.

"Yeah, well . . ." Heather shrugged again, as if she really didn't care.

Both adults could see clearly that she did.

Matt sighed. "All right, look. I haven't got time to go into it with you right now, but later in the week the three of us can get together and talk about it."

"What's to talk about?" Heather mumbled.

"Before I can help you, I need to know what I'm helping you with. You answer a few questions for me and I'll check into it and see what I can do. Maybe light a fire under your lawyer at Legal Aid. Okay? But only if I think your case warrants it," he added sternly, trying to avoid raising false hopes. "The courts grant emancipated-minor status only in very rare cases," he warned, "and I'm not about to add to an already overburdened system just because you don't get along with your parents. Is that clear?"

"Yeah, sure," Heather said with another unconcerned shrug, but her eyes were shining with hope.

Matt glanced at Susannah, expecting her to reinforce his statement of caution. She smiled back at him as if he were St. George about to slay the dragon. He sighed again, knowing when he was licked.

"Come on, Cinderella," he said, reaching for the wrap over her arm. He shook the deep-wine-colored velvet cape out and swirled it behind her, settling it on her shoulders. "Time to go to the ball."

6

A DARK-EYED, balding man with an affable smile and an intense manner swooped down on them the minute they entered the Peacock Court of the Mark Hopkins hotel. Or swooped down on Matt, rather. He didn't appear to notice Susannah at all.

"Where in hell's name have you been?" he said to Matt. "You're about to give me a heart attack! Councilman Leeland was asking about you a few minutes ago. And Mr. Hoi Lung Kwong wants to discuss your opinions on the recent court rulings regarding illegal immigration from China. Hell of a thing," he grumbled, "when the man of the hour is late."

"Susannah, this extremely rude man is Harry Gasparini, my campaign manager," Matt said calmly, unperturbed by the older man's air of impending doom. "Harry, this is Susannah Bennington. My date. And we are not late." He glance pointedly at his watch. "It's barely seven-thirty."

"Your date?" Harry's expression grew even more disapproving as he turned to stare at Susannah.

She smiled sweetly, showing lots of perfect white teeth.

"Bennington?" he said, obviously having trouble matching the woman standing before him with what he knew of the name. "Of Bennington Plastics?"

"My father is Roger Bennington, yes," she admitted.

"Then your mother must be Audrey Stanhope Bennington Harper?"

"Yes," Susannah said, surprised he'd made the connection that quickly. Not many people did.

Harry shook his head. "Never would have guessed it," he said, looking her up and down. His expression was not admiring.

"Thank you," Susannah said with another sugary-sweet smile. Her sarcasm was wasted. Harry had already turned his attention back to Matt.

"Come on over and say hello to the councilman," he said. "He's got some people he wants you to meet."

"Go on," Susannah said, clearly reading Matt's reluctance to leave her on her own in a room full of strangers. "I'll get myself a glass of champagne—" she summoned a passing waiter with the lift of an eyebrow "—and mingle. Maybe I'll run into your mother or Mr. Elliott."

"Wouldn't you like to meet the councilman?"

"I've met him," she said, lifting a glass of champagne off the waiter's tray. She'd been part of a committee that had lobbied the councilman's office in support of a bill for increased funding for battered women's shelters and police-sensitivity training in handling domestic-violence cases. The bill had been defeated, with Councilman Leeland heading up the opposition. "We had a slight disagreement a few years back." She took a sip of her champagne. "You go do your political duty," she said to Matt. "I'll meet up with you when it's time for dinner."

Susannah wandered around the edges of the crowd for the next half hour or so, deliberately keeping to the fringes of the groups that formed and reformed, listening in as people discussed politics, social change, the latest tabloid headlines, restaurants, movies, gay rights, their friends' affairs and what should be done about San Francisco's growing homeless problem.

"I think they should make those wretched people stay out of Union Square," said a voice Susannah recognized as Barbara Filbert's. "It's bad for the tourist trade. And it makes shopping so unpleasant."

Stupid cow, Susannah thought, edging away from that particular group before Mrs. Filbert noticed her.

"Did you see that latest Tom Cruise movie? I read he and his wife are going to—"

"He pleaded nolo contendere. I heard the judge threw the book at him anyway, though, so . . ."

"It's ridiculous to think that everyone can be covered by the same health plan. What about . . ."

"I heard that she caught him in the act. In flagrante delicto," the speaker said with relish. "Wouldn't you just love to have been a fly on the wall?"

"Some of those gay activists are going too far. Imagine, marrying each other!"

"God, isn't Matthew Ryan just the hunkiest thing you ever saw?" one young female politico said to another. "He makes you think about straying from the straight and narrow just so you could have him as a lawyer."

Susannah edged a little closer to listen to the conversation.

"He's a prosecuting attorney," her friend said. "He goes after criminals. He doesn't defend them."

"Well, he can come after me, anytime."

Me, too, Susannah thought. *Anytime at all.*

"My goodness. Susannah," said an all-too-familiar voice from behind her, "is that you?"

She turned around. "Hello, Mother." She leaned in for the obligatory kiss on the cheek. "How are you?"

"I'm fine." *Which you'd know if you came to visit more often.*

The words weren't spoken but Susannah heard them. "You look fine," she said, meaning it sincerely. Her mother was a beautiful woman. "I like what you've done with your hair. It's very attractive."

Audrey lifted a hand to smooth the coiffure that hadn't changed since Susannah was a child. "I had my hairdresser add a little drabber to the color this time. It was getting too brassy." She reached out and touched Susannah's springing corkscrew curls, trying to brush them back from her face. "You might want to try it on *your* hair next time you go in."

"I don't use anything on my hair but shampoo and conditioner, Mother," Susannah said dryly. Audrey was always trying to get her to use something to tone down her color. "You know that."

"Well . . ." Audrey looked her over consideringly. "Perhaps if you didn't insist on wearing such unsuitable colors your hair might not be so noticeable. There's a reason redheads shouldn't wear pink, you know."

"How's Brian?" Susannah asked. Brian was Audrey's husband. "Is he here tonight?"

"Oh, he's around here somewhere." She waved her hand languidly. "Talking business, as usual. He loves this sort of function." She gave her daughter a searching look. "I wouldn't have thought it would be your type of affair, though."

"No, it isn't," Susannah agreed. "I came with a friend."

"Oh?" Audrey gave her daughter an arch, inquiring look. "Anyone I know?"

Meaning, Susannah thought, *anyone worth knowing?* "No, I don't think you know him, Mother. Although I'm sure you've heard of his family. He's—"

She felt a hand at her back, on the bare skin just above the waistline of her dress. She started slightly but she didn't pull away; she knew exactly who it was. "They're going to start serving dinner in just few minutes, Susannah," Matt said into her ear. "We should find our table."

Susannah didn't know whether to be grateful he'd rescued her or appalled that her mother now knew who her friend was. Audrey would consider Matthew Ryan a bigger, better catch than that guy from three years ago—not that Susannah could blame her exactly. He *was* a better catch. But she wasn't trying to catch him.

"Aren't you going to introduce us, Susannah?"

"Yes, of course. Mother, this is Matthew Ryan. Matt, my mother, Audrey Stanhope Bennington Harper." Unlike most women who'd been divorced and remarried, Audrey had continued to use her first husband's name along with that of her new husband. She said it was because she wanted the connection with her daughter. Susannah thought it was because she didn't want anyone to forget her connection with Bennington Plastics.

"Mrs. Harper," Matt said politely. "It's a pleasure. I hope we get a chance to talk more after dinner. Susannah?" he said, indicating the direction she was to take with the hand on her back. "We're up near the podium."

"Of course." She hesitated long enough to lean forward and gave her mother another kiss on the cheek. "I'll see you later, Mother."

"Now I know who you were trying to imitate the other night," Matt whispered from behind her.

She glanced back over her shoulder at him. "Imitate?"

"The prim little black dress. The bun. You were playing dress-up with your mommy's clothes."

She stopped between the tables to turn around and confront him more directly. "Dress-up?" she said indignantly. "I'll have you know I dressed that way to put *your* mother at ease. It's my Nob Hill, society-matron disguise."

"Dress-up," Matt said. "But we can argue about it later." He put his hands on her shoulders and turned her around, then kept them there, steering her through the close-packed tables to the one nearest the podium.

"My, don't you look lovely, Susannah," Millicent Ryan said by way of greeting. "That's a stunning dress." She gazed up at her son. "Don't you think she looks stunning, Matthew?"

Matt surreptitiously ran a finger down Susannah's spine as he seated her. "Stunning," he said to his mother as he slipped into the seat between the two women.

Susannah pointedly ignored him, looking instead across both him and Millicent to the man sitting on the older woman's other side. "Mr. Elliott," she said warmly. "I'm glad you could make it."

"Do you two know each other?" Millicent asked.

"I meet this lovely young lady not long after I moved here from Iowa," Carlisle Elliott said with a twinkling smile.

Matt thought he looked a bit like Cesar Romero, as Susannah had said, only Anglo and not so tall. His hair was thick and almost pure white. His skin was weathered and deeply tanned. His tuxedo looked custom-made and his brightly patterned bow tie and cummerbund were of designer quality. Matt decided to run a background check on him the first thing in the morning.

"Susannah's been helping me get acquainted with my new city. Introducing me to people," Mr. Elliott said. "And I keep telling her to call me Carly."

"Carly," Susannah repeated obediently. "I take it you've already met Mrs. Ryan?"

"Oh, my, yes," said Millicent. "We've been sitting here having the nicest chat. Carly used to own a nursery in Iowa," she said to her son, "and you'll never guess what his specialty was. Roses!" she said, not waiting for him to guess. "Can you believe that?"

"Sounds like you two have a lot in common," Matt said. He reached around behind his mother and offered his hand to the older man. "I'm Matt Ryan, by the way. Millicent's son."

"Carlisle Elliott."

THE TALK AT THE TABLE became general after that. There were eight other people seated with them, mostly the captains of industry and political bigwigs Susannah had once accused Matt of knowing. One of them was Councilman Leeland. He looked at Susannah searchingly once or twice but never seemed able to place her. Fortunately, he was seated far enough away that conversation between them was impractical. The hotel kitchen proved more than equal to its reputation for fine French food, making for a superb meal. And then, finally, the dishes were cleared away and the real purpose of the evening was at hand.

Councilman Leeland spoke first, thanking everyone for coming and contributing so generously to the campaign coffers. He craftily pontificated on his own career and achievements first. He praised Matt's father next: his record and his rulings, his political savvy and know-how, his ability to get out there and get out the vote.

Then, finally, he got to the reason they were all there.

He started with Matt's outstanding scholastic record, his beginnings with the DA.'s office, his rapid rise and many successes, his most recent convictions. He touched on his fine legal mind, his spotless integrity, his dedication, his ferocity and tenacity when it came to prosecuting society's worst criminals, comparing it favorably with that of his father, who'd been known as a stern but fair judge.

Susannah sat next to Matt, listening to the accolades being heaped upon him, and wondered if the man Councilman Leeland was praising, this ruthless crusader for truth and justice, this dedicated public servant he spoke of could possibly be the man who sat beside her, playing with her fingers under the table.

Oh, she had no doubt he could be ruthless; he'd have to be to have attained the position he held. She knew he could be judgmental, skeptical and suspicious; she'd seen it in his reaction to Judy's past. But she also knew he was capable of compassion and tenderness; she'd seen that, too, in the way he'd dealt with Heather. And with her.

She wondered if any of the political pundits and society bigwigs saw him as she did. Did they see his compassion? His humor? His simple *humanness*? Or did they even consider those things important in the political scheme of things?

Her musings were interrupted when Councilman Leeland introduced the man of the hour, bringing him to the podium on a rousing swell of applause. Matt squeezed her hand under the table and rose to his feet, striding toward his destiny with firm, unhurried steps.

His speech was short and to the point. If elected, he promised to do his best to justify their faith in him and to execute his judicial responsibilities with as much fairness and impartiality as humanly possible. And then he thanked them all for their support and quit the podium.

The audience was a little stunned at the brevity of his speech but none could doubt its sincerity. And, as an added bonus, they all got to go home a little earlier.

It took another forty-five minutes for the crowd to disperse and the room to empty. Everyone wanted to come up and exchange a word or two with the candidate, some to express their support and their hopes for his success, some to lobby for future goodwill. Matt was unfailingly polite and gracious to everyone, but Susannah could sense his eagerness to be gone.

She wondered if it was simply too many hours in a crowded room that made him feel so restless, or whether it was something more serious and long-lasting. The weight of everyone's expectations, perhaps, or the burden of his father's legacy? Despite what he said, she still wasn't entirely convinced Matt wanted to be a judge.

He nudged her lightly with his elbow, jogging her out of her abstraction. "Ready to go?"

Susannah looked around the room. It was empty except for the two of them and half a dozen hotel staffers busily dismantling tables and stacking chairs. "Where's your mother?"

Matt gave her a crooked grin. "It looks like your matchmaking was a success this time. She accepted Elliott's offer to see her home."

Susannah grinned back. "See what a little one-on-one can accomplish?"

He held out his hand. "Let's go get your cape," he said, thinking about a little one-on-one he was going to pursue as soon as he got her back to his apartment.

THERE WAS NO ATTENDANT in the coatroom, an unusual occurrence at the Mark Hopkins. They waited for a moment or two, in case the attendant came back from wherever he had gone.

"Keep a lookout," Matt said playfully. "I'm going in."

Susannah waited for a few seconds, then a few seconds more, wondering what was taking him so long. How difficult could it be to find a velvet cape? Espe-

cially when the coatroom had to be very nearly empty.
She leaned over the counter, trying to see. "Matt? Can't
you find it?"

"What color is it?"

"Dark wine-red."

Another second or two of silence.

"I can't find it," he said. "You'd better come look."

Susannah sighed with amused exasperation. Men!
They all had some sort of hereditary, gender-specific
blindness when it came to things that were right in front
of them. She saw the cape as soon as she entered the
coatroom. "For goodness' sake, it's right—"

Her words were abruptly cut off as Matt yanked her
into his arms and pressed his mouth to hers. Susannah
forgot all about her cape. She wrapped her arms around
him and kissed him back, just as fiercely as he was
kissing her.

"God, I've been wanting to do that all night," Matt
breathed when he finally raised his head. "I couldn't
wait another minute to taste you. Not another second."

"Kiss me again," Susannah demanded fiercely. She
threaded her hands through his hair and pulled his head
down to hers.

Matt kissed her again. And then again. And again.
He ran his hands over the bodice of her dress, lightly,
aware of its delicacy, but fervently, too, looking for a
way under the heavily beaded chiffon. He settled, finally, for easing one of the fragile beaded straps down
to her biceps, nudging it gently until, finally, he could
ease his hand up under her arm and slide it inside the
bodice of her dress.

She wasn't wearing a bra. He didn't know why he would have thought she was, given the construction of the dress, but it hadn't even occurred to him that she might be bare under all that beading. He was glad he hadn't thought of it. He'd have gone stark, raving crazy during dinner if he'd thought of it. He wouldn't have been able to stand up and give his speech if he'd thought of it. He brushed his thumb over the underside of her breast, his fingers caressing the full upper curves. Her swollen nipple rested in the notch between his thumb and index finger. He squeezed gently.

Susannah moaned and pressed herself into his hand. He was driving her crazy! The ravenous demand of his mouth, hungry and hard, contrasted so deliciously with the delicate touch of his hand on her flesh. Passion and tenderness. Savagery and subtlety. The combination was more erotic than anything she'd ever experienced before.

She shifted her hold on him, running one hand down his side, slipping it between them to caress his penis. He was rock-hard and ready under her hand. She moaned again and squeezed him.

He responded by groaning like a man mortally wounded and backed her up against the wall between the coats. His hand left her breast, eased out from under her bodice and headed downward, gathering up the diaphanous layers of her skirt so he could reach what lay beneath. His questing fingers brushed over a lacy stocking top, and then he hesitated, shocked and delighted to discover the smooth bare skin of her thigh. He groaned again.

"Let's get a room," he whispered against her mouth. His voice was raspy with need and sexual desire.

"Yes," Susannah whispered, her voice as raspy as his.

"It'll take too long to get back to my place. And I can't wait." He kissed her again—deeply, erotically—and brushed his fingertips against the silk that guarded her most feminine secrets. "I don't want to wait."

Susannah's whole body tensed at the delicate, butterfly caress. "Yes," she said again. "I can't wait, either. I don't want to wait. I—"

"He's a little resistant to a heavy campaign schedule but I can wo—Jesus H. Christ!" Harry Gasparini's curse bounced off the walls of the coatroom like a Ping-Pong ball gone wild, ricocheting around the two people locked in a torrid embrace. "What the hell's going on in here?" he demanded.

It was a purely rhetorical question. Any damn fool could see what was going on.

Susannah closed her eyes and hid her face in Matt's shoulder. Matt tensed and turned his body to better shield her from sight. "Give us a minute, please, Harry," he said quietly.

But Harry wasn't about to be so easily dismissed. "You just about gave me a goddamned heart attack," he complained. "What the hell were you think—"

"*Now*, Harry," Matt said in a voice that brooked no argument. He waited until he heard the muffled sound of retreating footsteps, then eased his fierce hold on the woman in his arms.

Susannah looked up at him. "He wasn't alone," she said.

He raised an eyebrow.

"Councilman Leeland."

"Ah, well," he said, reaching to lift her beaded strap back into place on her shoulder. "It could be worse."

She eyed him skeptically.

"It could have been my mother. Or yours. Or—" he smiled wickedly "—Barbara Filbert."

"That isn't funny," Susannah said. But she giggled. "Oh, God, don't get me started. This isn't anything to laugh about."

Matt shook his head. "The only possible response to a situation like this is laughter."

"But your career. Your campaign. The newspapers will have a field day with this."

"With what?" he asked reasonably. "I'm not married. You're not married. They didn't catch me in here with a guy. Or by myself." He smiled teasingly and Susannah couldn't help but smile in return. "So what can they say? Assistant DA. Matthew Ryan was caught in a passionate clinch with a gorgeous woman? They might question my judgment as regards to time and place. If they knew about it." He shrugged. "Which they won't because Harry certainly isn't going to tell anyone. Nor will Leeland. It'd be counterproductive to the campaign."

"You find your coats yet?" Harry called loudly, more loudly than he needed to.

"The attendant must be back," Matt said. "I found it," he hollered back, grabbing Susannah's cape off the hanger just as the attendant entered the coatroom.

"I'm sorry I wasn't here, Mr. Ryan," he apologized. "I didn't think I'd be gone that long. I hope you weren't too inconvenienced."

"Not at all," Matt assured him as he settled the cape around Susannah's shoulders. He pulled it close around her, smiling into her eyes as he freed her hair and then tied the velvet cords under her chin. "No inconvenience at all."

He reached into his pants pocket as they left the coatroom, extracting the folded bills he'd put there earlier, and casually dropped Heather's fifteen dollars into the tip basket as he passed it. Those few moments of heated intimacy in the coatroom would have been a bargain at twice the price.

MATT FASTENED his seat belt and reached for the ignition key. "Come home with me?" he said, glancing over at his passenger.

"I shouldn't."

"Probably not."

"You know that old saying about politics making strange bedfellows?" she asked him. "That's us. We're crazy if we take this any further. Absolutely mad."

"Very likely."

"I'm against the death penalty."

"I figured you probably were," Matt said, understanding the seeming non sequitur perfectly. He'd publicly stated he was in favor of it for specific crimes.

"I'm a liberal Democrat," she elaborated, thinking that perhaps he hadn't quite understood. "Very liberal."

"And I'm a middle-of-the-road Republican. So? It could get a little loud if we decide to talk politics but it's not exactly the Capulets and Montagues."

"I'm for stringent gun-control laws."

"Within reason," he agreed.

"I believe there's no such thing as a bad boy. Or girl."

"A little naive, but praiseworthy."

"I think there should be term limits for most elected offices so men like Councilman Leeland can't obstruct progress for years and years."

"I can understand that." He waited for a beat. "Anything else?"

"I think gays should have equal rights under the law. And that women have the right to choose. I think the term *family values* should apply to all families, not just the traditional mommy-daddy-and-two-kids kind. I don't believe in the trickle-down theory of economics. I do believe that Bush knew about Iran-Contra." She slanted a glance at him out of the corner of her eye. "I think each state should have one male and one female senator."

Matt's eyebrow rose. "Mandated by law?"

"If that's what it takes to get fair and equal representation."

Matt shook his head. "Well, I admit, I'd have to argue that last one with you, but we agree on the rest. Is that it?"

Susannah considered for a moment. "Yes, that's pretty much it. We don't have enough in common to start a civil conversation. And even if by some miracle, we *did* manage to build some kind of relationship, it wouldn't last."

"How do you figure that?"

"I wouldn't be good for your career, Matt. I don't mean because of what happened tonight. Passion like that will burn itself out, sooner or later." She waved her hand, brushing aside the objection she sensed he was about to make. "I mean in the long run. I'm not a political helpmate. I'm not docile. Or unassuming. I won't sit back and keep my mouth shut if some jackass says something I disagree with. Not for long, anyway. And if someone asks me for my opinion, I'll give it to him, even if it's different from yours. I'm not inconspicuous and I don't want to be. My mother tried to make me all those things when I was growing up—and you can see how well *that* worked."

Matt couldn't stop the grin that tugged at his lips. "Sweetheart, you couldn't be inconspicuous if you tried."

"Well, there, you see? I'm right. It would never work."

He just looked at her. "Come home with me tonight?"

"Yes."

7

MATT'S CONDOMINIUM apartment was only ten blocks away from the hotel, tucked into one of the narrow residential streets in the Russian Hill district of the city. The facade was a pleasant mix of traditional San Francisco bay windows and modern redwood siding. The interior was uncluttered and elegant, with comfortable furniture in pale grays and blues with occasional accents of dark navy and deep chrome yellow. Paintings crowded the walls.

The pieces were strikingly varied: some modern abstracts that were mere slashes of color, some dreamy nudes, several San Francisco cityscapes that Susannah recognized as having been painted by local artists and a few delicately rendered Japanese watercolors. There were three sculptures, too, each sitting atop its own softly lighted display column. Two were sinuous, shiny metal forms that begged to be touched. The third was made of thick sea-blue glass curved into an abstract evocation of a cresting wave. Somehow, it all worked.

"You collect?" Susannah asked, surprised and entranced by this side of him.

"Not really," Matt answered, watching her move around the room, viewing his art collection. He shivered as she ran a fingertip over the curve of the glass wave. "I just buy what I like and hang it on the walls."

Susannah untied the velvet ties of her cape and shrugged out of it, pausing for a moment to drape it over the back of the sofa. The beads on the bodice of her dress glimmered even in the low light, shimmering enticingly with each movement of the slender body under it.

Matt took a deep breath and told himself to be patient; they had the whole night ahead of them. "Would you like a brandy?"

Susannah turned her head to look at him. "No, thank you."

"Coffee?"

"No." She shook her head. "Nothing."

Matt suddenly couldn't wait any longer. "Would you like to make love with me?" he said, low.

Susannah's smile was tremulous. "Yes, please."

He held out his hand and she put hers in it.

They walked down a short hall and up a flight of stairs to his bedroom. It was spare and elegant, furnished with a low platform bed, a teak dresser and a wooden chair of sleek Scandinavian design. One entire wall was made up of floor-to-ceiling shelves and cupboards, with places for books, framed photographs, various small objets d'art and an extensive state-of-the-art audio/video system. Another wall, and nearly a third of the sloping ceiling, was made up of large rectangular panes of glass. The windows looked out over a patch of nature, a small copse of mature trees and shrubs, one of the unexpected delights often found in the middle of the city's residential districts. Farther out, past the trees, the lights of San Francisco twinkled in the darkness. Farther still lay the midnight black waters of the bay.

"Shall I close the blinds?" Matt asked, watching her hungrily. He'd been thinking of her here, in his bedroom, for what seemed like forever, yet less than three weeks had passed since that day in her office. It was hard to believe she was really here, now. Harder still to make himself take things slow.

"No. Leave them open," she said, staring out at the magnificent view. "It's beautiful."

"Yes," he said. "It is."

She turned her head, meeting his eyes, and smiled at the compliment.

Matt felt his stomach muscles clench with the need to toss her down on the bed and bury himself in her sweet flesh.

"How about some music?" he said, moving purposefully toward the wall unit. He inserted a CD into the player without paying much attention to what it was, and jabbed the *on* button. Something soft and soulful, with lots of sax, filled the room. Matt held out his arms. "Dance with me, Susannah."

She floated into his embrace, as soft as an angel, as fragrant as a flower, as sweet as the Sugarplum Fairy, as naturally seductive as Eve at the dawn of time. Holding her in his arms was both heaven and hell. He wanted to make the evening last, to make it good for her, to linger over every nuance of the experience and her reaction to it. He wanted to be inside her, *now*, hot and hard, pounding his way to completion in the exquisite softness of her body.

She stirred in his embrace and pressed closer, nuzzling her cheek against his shoulder as they swayed to the music. She could feel the strength in his arms, hard and tense around her, and in his chest, solid and warm against her breasts, and in his erection, rigid against the softness of her belly. She could feel the restraint, the leashed power, just waiting to explode into passion.

She appreciated what he was attempting to do. The romance. The gentle wooing. The slow climb to passion. It was sweet and thoughtful but so unnecessary. She didn't need the trappings of romance tonight; she didn't even want them.

She wanted the passion and the power she sensed in him. The hardness and the heat he held pressed against her. She wanted his hunger, unleashed and unrestrained. Man to her woman. Elemental. Basic. Wild.

She raised her head. "Kiss me," she demanded.

Matt groaned. "If I do that, I'm going to lose control and end up ripping this pretty dress right off your body."

She gave him a slow, witchy smile. A woman's smile, full of temptation and promises. "I guess I'd better take my dress off then, hadn't I?"

Matt groaned again.

Susannah lifted her left arm. "The zipper's right there. See? It's hidden in the seam."

Matt grasped the little metal tab between his finger and thumb and pulled gently, careful not to catch the delicate chiffon in the zipper's teeth. The heavy beaded fabric fell away from her body as the pressure that held it was released, leaving a wide gap from just under her arm to the flare of her hip where the beaded bodice of the dress met the filmy skirt. Matt ran the backs of his fingers up her bare side, leaving gooseflesh in his wake. "You feel like silk," he breathed. His voice shook with the force of his passion.

Susannah shivered, feeling lush and seductive and uncontestably, irresistibly female. It was a wonderful way to feel, she decided. A perfectly delicious way to feel.

She wanted more.

She stepped back, out of his embrace. Reaching up, she placed one hand between her breasts to hold the fabric in place and slowly, watching his face the whole time, slipped one beaded strap, and then the other, off her shoulders.

Matt started forward, his hands out, reaching for her. Susannah shook her head and stepped back, stopping him dead in his tracks without a word.

"Susannah," he choked out. Perspiration beaded on his upper lip. A small muscle jerked in his clenched jaw. His fingers flexed. But he didn't move.

Still holding the bodice to her breasts, still watching his face, she eased one arm, and then the other, completely out of the straps. Then, with a seductive little wiggle, she lifted her hand and let go of the dress. Weighted by the heavy beading, it slid all the way to the floor, leaving her clad in gossamer thigh-high stockings with lace tops, high-heeled shoes and pale ivory silk tap pants. She took another step back, out of the circle of fabric at her feet.

They stared at each other for a long moment. Her, nearly naked, soft, curved, womanly, her breasts full and aching, the nipples tight, her body quivering in anticipation. Him, fully clothed, hot, hard, painfully aroused, his raw male power barely hidden behind the civilized facade of the elegant tuxedo he wore.

The contrast was tantalizing. Exciting. Overwhelmingly, irresistibly, unbearably erotic.

Susannah straightened her shoulders and lifted her chin in mute feminine challenge, looking at him out of heavy-lidded, luminous eyes. "Now," she said, releasing him.

It was like unleashing a force of nature.

He came at her with a low growl, his hands out, reaching. She felt his fingers bite into her waist and then she was propelled backward, lifted off of her feet for a moment—losing her shoes in the process—before he slammed her down on the quilted navy bedspread. He was on her immediately, and all over her. Everywhere. His hands caressing and stroking feverishly. His mouth blindly seeking, pressing hot, open-mouthed kisses randomly over her bare flesh until he found the prize he sought.

His lips closed over her nipple, avid and greedy to taste and possess but exquisitely careful not to be *too* rough. He sucked hard and deep. And then more softly, using his tongue to tease and caress. And then hard again, using his whole mouth.

Subtlety and savagery, Susannah thought. White-hot passion and exquisite tenderness. It was a potent combination.

She moaned and arched voluptuously, pushing her breast more deeply into his mouth. She ran her hands over his shoulders and back impatiently, frustrated by her inability to touch the bare skin she suddenly craved with an intensity she'd never felt before. She curled her hands over the collar of his tuxedo jacket and pushed it down, trying to ease it off his shoulders. He shrugged out of it impatiently, one arm at a time, uncaring that it landed in a crumpled heap at the foot of the bed as he shook it off.

Susannah reached for the studs on his shirt next, intent on getting down to bare skin, but his position was wrong and he was unaware of what she was trying to do. Intent on gratifying his own driving need to touch what was covered, he curled his fingers into the fabric at the side of her fragile panties and yanked. They tore easily, coming away in one ragged piece. He tossed them aside without a thought and delved between her thighs with eager fingers.

She was hot and wet and slick, as swollen as if she'd been ready and aroused for hours. She cried out, her whole body quivering in helpless reaction when his fingers merely brushed against her tumid clitoris. The sound drove him wild.

He lifted himself off her, just far enough to reach between their bodies and yank open the fastenings at the front of his trousers. He pushed his trousers and underpants down over his hips and his erection sprang free, hot and hard, quivering against the sensitive skin of Susannah's thigh.

She whimpered and lifted her knees, offering him what they both wanted before he could move to take it. He shifted, poised to enter her and then swore savagely and pulled back.

Susannah grabbed at his bare hips to keep him where he was.

"Condom," he said between gritted teeth. His whole body was shaking with the need to sink into her. "Goddamned condom is in the drawer."

He stretched out his arm, trying to reach the nightstand, but they were too far down on the bed. He curled his other arm under her waist and lifted, dragging her with him, still under him, as he moved on hand and knees toward the nightstand. Susannah used her heels, pushing against the mattress for added leverage when she realized what he was doing. Because of the position they were in and the way they were moving—Susannah pushing and arching her body, Matt stretching and straining—those parts of them which were most basically male and female bumped against each other in delicious, maddening counterpoint, heightening the urgency to reach their goal.

Matt's rough laughter sounded in her ear. "God, we must look like a couple of sex-crazed idiots," he said.

"I know." She giggled breathlessly and then stiffened as his shaft brushed against her most sensitive flesh. "But hurry."

His fingers reached the drawer pull and he yanked it open.

"Hurry," Susannah said again as he fumbled with the little foil packet.

But his hands were shaking too badly to manage it.

She reached up and took it from him, tearing it open with her teeth. Then, while he balanced above her on hands and knees, she unrolled it onto his turgid length. It was one of the most erotic acts of her life.

He sank down onto her then, into her, entering her in a controlled rush, sinking into her to the hilt, stretching her, filling her to overflowing. Susannah planted her heels against the mattress and lifted herself into it, deepening his possession, demanding all of him. He probed her deeply, slowly grinding his groin against hers in an effort to make it last as long as possible. His big hands cradled her head, holding her still for a kiss as carnal as the act itself.

Susannah ran her hands down his back, seeking the bare flesh of his tight male buttocks, and pressed him closer.

He groaned into her mouth and ground his hips into her.

She tore her mouth from his, planting a row of tiny, hot kisses in a line to his ear. "Harder," she breathed raggedly, and pressed her nails into his buttocks. "Faster."

Matt shivered and stilled, his control pushed to the very edge by her passionate demand.

"Go on," she whispered. "Take me the way I know you're dying to. I want you to."

He lifted his head to look at her. "For pity's sake, Susannah," he growled through gritted teeth, "show a little sense."

She tightened her inner muscles around him in answer.

He groaned and his hips flexed convulsively against hers, driving her down into the mattress. "If I just take what I want, I'm going to leave you behind," he ground out.

Susannah smiled that witchy, womanly smile. "No, you won't," she purred and rubbed the back of her stocking-clad calf against his hip.

Because he desperately wanted to believe it, Matt took her at her word. He slipped his hands under her, sliding them down to cup her buttocks, cushioning and supporting her for a more vigorous penetration.

"Yes," Susannah moaned when he began to thrust harder and faster against her. "Yes." The feeling was exquisite, building higher, spiraling, tightening until she thought she would faint from the intensity. But she didn't faint, she locked her ankles at the small of his back and reached up behind her to grasp the headboard instead, bracing herself to take even more of him. "Yes, yes, yes, yes . . ." she began to chant in time with each of his powerful thrusts, glorying in his desperate, frantic need of her. *"Yes!"*

Her climax shook her powerfully, just seconds before his claimed him, hurling her headlong into a whirlwind of intemperate feeling and wondrous sensation, leaving her weak and drained and feeling gloriously, giddily replete. She felt curiously euphoric and light, like a bright red balloon bobbing on the end of a string.

Matt was still for a long moment, his breath rasping against her neck and then he heaved a deep, ragged sigh and levered himself up on to his elbows. "You okay?" he asked, brushing back her tangle of corkscrew curls.

She smiled up at him. "I'm fantastic."

"You are that," Matt agreed. He kissed her nose and lifted himself off her, discreetly disposing of the condom before collapsing onto his back at her side.

She turned her head to look at him. His pale blond hair was damp around the edges. His sharp Nordic cheekbones were flushed. His wide chest was still heaving beneath the pin-tucked pleats of his white dress shirt. And his pants were bunched around his ankles, held in place by the shoes he'd been in too much of a frenzy to remove.

He grinned at her, his blue eyes glowing with satisfaction and masculine triumph. And a certain particular joy he'd never felt before. "As soon as I get my breath back we're going to do this again," he said, reaching over to snap the elasticized lace top of her stocking.

THEY DID IT twice more, in fact, once on the bathroom floor when they went in to take a shower and once up against the inside of his front door. They were on their way out that final time, Susannah dressed once again in her evening finery.

Matt was never quite sure, later, what it was that set him off. Maybe it was the mere sight of her. Maybe it was the way she turned her head to smile at him as she reached for the doorknob. Maybe it was because she was leaving and he didn't want her to go. Maybe it was just knowing she didn't have anything on under her dress.

Whatever it was, he was rock-hard in a second, as avid and hungry as if they hadn't just made love thirty minutes before. He put his hand on her arm, turning her around, and backed her up against the door with his body.

She lifted a teasing eyebrow. "And what do you think you're doing, Counselor Ryan?" she said playfully, putting her hands on his shoulders as if to hold him off.

His growled response was hot, sexy and graphic.

Susannah's hands went slack on his shoulders for a moment and then she slid them around his neck and stretched up for his kiss, suddenly as hungry as he was.

It happened fast.

Their mouths met in an avid, eating kiss. A kiss that was deep and carnal and blatantly erotic. His tongue moved in and out of her mouth and she sucked at it greedily. His hands slid down to her hips, gathering up the layers of her skirt to get at the treasure between her legs. She jerked his belt buckle and lowered the zipper on his khaki chinos to get at his. His hands curled under her buttocks, opening her legs to his caress. Her fingers slid inside his Jockey shorts, freeing his erection into her hands. He lifted her, his hands on the back of her thighs, the weight of his chest holding her against the door, and surged forward, his body seeking entrance to hers. She locked her legs around his waist and her arms around his neck and accepted him into her. One stroke . . . two . . . three . . . four, and they both exploded in a white-hot swirl of ecstasy unlike anything either of them had ever known before.

The trembling aftermath lasted longer than the act itself. They came back slowly, gradually, with baby-soft kisses and gentle nuzzling and sweet sighs of satisfaction. Susannah's legs grew lax and she let her feet drift back to the floor. Matt eased his weight off her, no longer needing to hold her up against the door. They stood there for long minutes, their arms still wrapped around each other and their hearts pressed together. Her face was tucked into his neck, his cheek rested on her hair. Contentment enveloped them like a San Francisco fog.

And then Matt raised his head and cupped her cheek in his palm, gently turning her face up to his. He waited until she opened her eyes and smiled at him.

"What?" she murmured sleepily, and rubbed her cheek against his hand.

"I think I've fallen in love with you," he said.

Susannah's eyes flared wide. "Matt," she said softly, stunned.

"No, not think," Matt interrupted, correcting himself before she could form the words to answer him. "I am in love with you." He lifted his other hand to her cheek, cradling her face between his wide palms as he stared down into her eyes. "I want you to marry me, Susannah."

8

"AFTER YOU'VE FINISHED with that, see what you can dig up on a girl called Heather Lloyd," Matt said to his assistant. "She's a juvenile. About sixteen. Social Services probably has a file on her. And check with Legal Aid. She's using one of their staffers to file for emancipated-minor status. I want a full report on her case as soon as you can manage it, without neglecting anything else, okay?"

"Okay." The young black woman nodded her understanding. When Matt Ryan said he wanted a full report as soon as possible, he meant yesterday, no matter how polite the request. "Anything else?"

"I want you to run a basic background check on a Carlisle Elliott. He's sixty-four. Used to own a nursery business someplace in Iowa. He sold it about six months ago and retired to live on a houseboat in Sausalito. Drives a red Corvette," Matt said with a bemused shake of his head. He rattled off the license-plate number.

"Priority?"

"The highest." He flashed a sheepish grin at her from across the desk. "My mother's planning to go out with him."

The young woman grinned back. "And you want to make sure his intentions are honorable?"

"Something like that."

The intercom on his desk sounded. "Mr. Gasparini's here to see you, Matt," the receptionist informed him. "Shall I send him up?"

"Yeah, tell him to come on up." He looked back at his assistant. "Is there anything else we need to cover right now, Gail?"

"Nothing that can't wait. For a few minutes, anyway." She pointed at his In box. "The latest statements from our star witness—" she said the last two words disparagingly "—in the Delaney case are on top of that stack. She changed her story again."

"What does that make it? The third time?"

Gail nodded.

He picked the file up and handed it across the desk to her. "Give this back to Parker," he said. "Tell him to put the pressure on. See if a loss of immunity does anything for her memory. I don't want to see that again," he added, nodding at the file in her hand, "until it's been settled. I'm not taking this case to court with a witness who can't make up her mind about what she saw. Make sure Parker understands my position."

"Sure thing, Matt." She stood up as the door to his office opened. "Mr. Gasparini," she said, nodding pleasantly at Matt's campaign manager. "You're due back in court at two-fifteen," she said to Matt, the reminder as much for Matt's visitor as for her boss. She exited the office, pulling the door closed behind her.

Matt waved a hand toward the chair in front of his desk. "So what's on your mind, Harry?" he asked, as if he didn't already know.

"Susannah Bennington," Harry said bluntly, getting right to the point.

"My relationship with Susannah Bennington isn't up for discussion."

"Dammit, Matt. You're running for office. Your whole life is up for discussion."

Matt sighed, knowing it was true. "All right, what about Susannah?"

"You serious about her? Or was that little love fest in the coatroom just a bit of slap and tickle?" It was obvious from Harry's expression that he hoped it was the latter.

"Serious enough that I've asked her to marry me," Matt said.

"Jesus H. Christ! Marriage? You're giving me a heart attack here!"

Matt raised an eyebrow. "Yeah," he said, amused, "that was pretty much her reaction, too."

"She turned you down?" The expression on Harry's face was one of renewed hope.

"She didn't mean it," Matt said, confident that her final answer would be yes. It *had* to be yes.

"You wanna be a little more specific here?"

"What specifics do you want, Harry? I asked her to marry me. She said no. I plan to keeping asking her until she says yes. Is that specific enough for you?"

"You wanna tell me why?"

"Why what?"

"Why her?"

Matt shrugged. "Hell, Harry, why does anybody want to marry anybody? I'm in love with her, that's why."

"It doesn't sound as if she's in love with you."

"Yes." Matt nodded. If he knew anything about Susannah, he knew that. "She is. She's just afraid she'll hurt my chances for a political career."

"She's right," Harry said earnestly. "She'll ruin you, Matt."

"Be careful, Harry," Matt warned softly. "You're talking about the woman I love."

"I'm only telling you the truth," Harry said. "Just like she obviously tried to tell you. The woman isn't right for you. She's got a record, for one thing."

"A record?" Matt said, diverted by that bit of information. Susannah hadn't mentioned anything about a record. "What kind of record?"

"Protest marches. Civil disobedience. That kind of thing. The woman's a bleeding-heart liberal!" It was the worst thing Harry could say about anyone. "She was a rabble-rouser at Berkeley."

Matt hadn't known she'd gone to Berkeley—that most liberal of liberal colleges—but the information didn't surprise him.

"A rabble-rouser when she worked for the county," Harry continued. "Always stirring up trouble one way or another. Always bucking the system. Hell, she's got a hooker working for her over at that dating service of hers."

"Ex-hooker," Matt said, feeling obligated to defend Judy in Susannah's absence.

"And she's got some hard-case juvenile delinquent living with her."

Matt grinned. Heather Lloyd was a hard case, all right.

"It's not funny, Matt. This is your political career we're talking about here."

Matt shook his head. "This is my life we're talking about here," he corrected. "And if it looks like the two can't be reconciled—" he looked Harry straight in the eye "—then maybe it's time I reassessed my priorities."

Harry changed tactics. "All right, hold on. There's no need to make any hasty decisions here, Matt. Let me look into the situation a little more. See what I can do to dress her up for the press."

Matt shook his head. "Susannah doesn't need to be dressed up for anyone. She is who she is. I mean it, Harry," he warned. "I don't want her upset or made to feel uncomfortable. And if I hear that she has been . . ." He shrugged and spread his hands. "I know my father trusted you to run his campaign the way you thought it should be run. I trust you, too. But Susannah isn't part of my campaign. Leave her out of it."

"She's out of it," Harry assured him, backpedaling for all he was worth. "Totally. I won't mention her again."

"I'm glad we could agree on this," Matt said. "I'd hate to lose you as my manager." He stood up and walked around the desk, reaching for the suit jacket hanging on the back of his office door. "Come on, I'll walk you out." He slipped into the jacket. "I have to be in court in twenty minutes."

MATT SAT with one hip on the edge of Susannah's desk, having basically the same conversation with her that he'd had with his campaign manager earlier that same day. The only difference was that it was much nicer arguing with Susannah. The view was better, for one thing. And he had something besides paperwork to keep his hands occupied.

"You're making mountains out of molehills," he said cajolingly. "Seeing problems where none exist."

"Yet," Susannah added stubbornly, refusing to be cajoled.

Matt laughed ruefully. "You're as bad as Harry." He removed one hand from her waist and lifted it to her chin, gently forcing her to meet his gaze. "What could possibly happen at a simple Fourth of July picnic?"

"Nothing. *If* it was just a simple picnic. But you and I both know it's not. It's a cleverly disguised campaign rally."

"It's a Fourth of July picnic in Golden Gate Park."

"Your campaign manager will be there, won't he? And Councilman Leeland? And lots of potential voters?"

"All right," Matt said, exasperated. He dropped his hand back to her waist, holding her so she couldn't move away. "You caught me. So it's a campaign rally. I'm going to make a speech, shake a few hands, maybe kiss a few babies, and I want you there with me." A crafty light entered his blue eyes. "Think of it as a golden opportunity," he suggested. "A chance to prove to me that you're right and I'm wrong."

She eyed him suspiciously.

"You say you won't fit into my world. I say you would." He waggled her back and forth with his hands at her waist. "This is your chance to show me."

She tilted her head, looking up at him from under her lashes with a considering light in her eyes. Maybe he had a point. Maybe—

The phone trilled, interrupting her train of thought. She glanced over at it, waiting for someone in the outer office to pick it up. When it rang a second time, Matt reached around behind him on the desk and picked up the receiver. He put it to her ear.

"The Personal Touch," she said, smiling into his eyes as she reached up to take the receiver into her own hand. "How may I help you?" The smile in her eyes vanished into a frown. "No," she said, annoyance plain in her voice. "You've got the wrong number." She reached around Matt and dropped the receiver into its cradle with a bang.

Matt raised an eyebrow.

"I swear," Susannah said in a tone of half-amused exasperation, "there must be a losers' convention in town this week. That's the third call like that today." She shook her head. "The jerk wanted, and I quote, 'a leggy redhead with big knockers,' unquote."

Matt couldn't help but grin at her indignation. "Maybe he didn't have the wrong number, after all," he said, unable to resist teasing her.

She eyed him warily.

He slid his hands up her torso to her breasts. "I don't think these quite qualify as 'knockers,'" he said consideringly, cupping his hands around her gentle curves. "But you've got the legs. And the hair is definitely red."

Susannah bit back a smile. "You're asking for it," she warned him.

"Uh-huh," he agreed, nodding eagerly. "Am I gonna get it?"

Unable to resist, she moved deeper into his embrace and offered her lips. He took them eagerly. Tenderly. Thoroughly. Long delicious minutes later, he broke the kiss, drawing back slightly to look into her eyes. "So," he said, fighting down the desire to lay her out on the desk and make mad, passionate love to her. "Are you going to go to the picnic with me? To test out our compatibility as a couple in public?"

"It'll be a real test?" she said. "No pulling punches? I can be completely myself?"

"I wouldn't have it any other way."

"No safe little preppie outfit? No pretending I haven't got any opinions of my own?"

He nodded. "No being outrageous just for the sake of being outrageous, either," he said, adding a condition of his own.

"Okay. You're on."

SUSANNAH HAD A hard time deciding what to wear to the Fourth of July picnic. The first outfit she put together was too drab and conservative, making her fear she was already compromising herself in an unconscious effort to fail her own test.

The second outfit she tried on went too far in the other direction, making her look like a refugee from Hollywood's version of a gypsy camp and, thus, violating Matt's stipulation against outrageousness simply for the sake of outrageousness. She took it off, throwing it across the bed on top of the first outfit.

Susannah eyed the resulting combination consider-ingly.

Perfect, she decided.

The cream-colored tunic sweater from the first out-fit, the gauzy, multicolored, midcalf skirt from the sec-ond. She added a pair of flat, strappy sandals, large gold hoop earrings and a blue scrunchie to hold her hair loosely at her nape.

It was definitely her.

"DO YOU EVEN *OWN* A PAIR of jeans?" she said to Matt, glancing over at him as they walked, hand in hand, from the parked car to the picnic area. He was wearing pressed tan chinos—with a *crease*, for goodness' sake!—and a pale blue polo shirt that, admittedly, showed off an impressive chest and did wonderful things for his eyes. He'd left his sport jacket in the car at her suggestion.

"Did I criticize what you're wearing?" he asked mildly.

"I'm not criticizing. I'm just asking. Do you?"

"One pair. Maybe," he added. "I think I might have worn them to stain the deck last year."

Susannah shook her head. It was too bad, really, be-cause he had the kind of compact little rear end that would look spectacular in a pair of tight-fighting 501s. "Did you want to criticize what I'm wearing?" she asked, suddenly realizing what he'd said.

He let his gaze sweep over her long, flowing skirt and cotton boat-necked sweater. He didn't quite under-stand why women were hiding their bodies in such loose, baggy clothes this season—especially when the woman in question had a body like Susannah's—but she looked fine to him. Lovely, in fact. He said as much. "Although I did wonder..." He let his voice trail off.

"What?" she demanded.

"Are you wearing anything under that outfit?"

She laughed and gave him an arch, sliding look out of the corners of her eyes. "Maybe, if you're a *really* good boy, I'll let you find out for yourself. Later," she said, silently resolving to remove her panties before that happened.

It would drive him crazy to think she'd gone all day without any underwear. *Men are so easily distracted,* she thought delightedly. All it took was some naked flesh, or even just the thought of it, and their fantasies were off and running.

THE PICNIC WAS being held near Stow Lake, the largest in Golden Gate Park, and the activities of the day were already under way by the time Matt and Susannah arrived.

Several men were marking the lanes and finish line for the traditional races—sack, three-legged, wheelbarrow and egg-and-spoon—while a couple of harried-looking teenagers rode herd on a group of smaller children, apparently trying to keep them away from the irresistible lure of the lake until the organized games could get under way. Women were gathered around one of the picnic tables, laughing and talking as they set out containers of food and handed out soft drinks to thirsty children. A uniformed cook, hired by the campaign committee, manned the smoking grills.

The smell of charcoal fires and barbecuing meat mingled with the scents of new-mown grass, rhododendrons and fresh air. A radio tuned to the play-by-play announcement of a big league baseball game competed with the blare of a golden-oldies station belting out sixties rock tunes.

A woman played a gentle game of catch with a toddler under a shade tree; teenagers flirted over a spirited game of croquet; a group of grade-school boys and girls kicked a soccer ball around a circle; a blue Frisbee sailed through the air.

Another group of people were gathered around a picnic table set a little away from the rest of the picnickers, so that their conversation wasn't infringed upon by the noise and laughter going on around them. Susannah recognized them instantly. They were the movers-and-shakers. The bigwigs. The politicians.

"Don't they ever let up?" Susannah mumbled as Councilman Leeland separated himself from the group and came toward them.

She could tell, as he ambled over to greet them, that he'd finally realized who she was. Whether he'd recognized her on his own, or Harry Gasparini had clued him in, really didn't matter, she decided, and steeled herself for a confrontation.

"Glad you could make it," he said to Matt, reaching out to give him a hearty handshake. "And you, too, little lady," he said to Susannah, leaning forward as if to kiss her cheek. She stepped back and stuck out her hand instead, forcing him to treat her as an equal. It disconcerted him for a moment, but he recovered quickly, pumping her hand as heartily as he had Matt's.

Sexist old goat, she thought, glancing up at Matt to see how he'd reacted to her maneuver.

He grinned at her.

"WHAT'S WRONG with a five-day waiting period to buy a gun?" Susannah said in exasperation, as she stood, half-surrounded by the men and women who were backing Matt's campaign. "A background check might not keep criminals from getting all the guns they want, but it would keep people like John Hinckley or that man who shot up that McDonald's a few years ago from getting their hands on a weapon. Both those men had serious mental problems that would have come to light with a mandatory background check."

"And what about legitimate gun collectors and hunters?" Councilman Leeland demanded, obviously doing his best to remain calm. "What about a decent, God-fearing citizen who just might want a gun for protection?"

"Well, what about them?" Susannah said. "A five-day waiting period isn't going to cause them anything but a little inconvenience. And if they haven't got a criminal record or a history of mental-health problems, why should they care if someone checks a file and doesn't find anything?"

"Because it violates their constitutional rights, that's why," the councilman said. "Our constitution grants every citizen the right to bear arms."

"Actually," Matt said, deciding it was time to add his two cents' worth to the argument, "it grants a 'duly appointed militia' the right to bear arms. I seriously doubt our illustrious forefathers intended every Tom, Dick and Harry to run around the countryside, brandishing a handgun."

Both Councilman Leeland and Susannah looked at him with open astonishment, although for vastly different reasons.

"Why so surprised?" Matt said to Susannah. "I told you I believed in reasonable gun control."

"Well," the councilman huffed. "Well. I think I'm going to have to talk to Harry about this development."

SUSANNAH HALF SAT, half stood, with her hips braced back against the short end of a picnic bench, sated by both the picnic food and the political speeches that had followed the open-air feast. Her legs were crossed at the ankles, the heels of her hands resting lightly on the wooden table on either side of her as she watched Matt work the crowd.

He was good, she thought proudly, her eyes misting up a little as she watched him. His manner was easy and natural, assuming leadership without any off-putting arrogance. He stated his views in simple language and responded to a direct question with a direct answer. When asked, he pointed out his opponents' shortcomings without resorting to personal attacks of any kind. He made them laugh. He made them like him. He made them believe he would do his best. And do the right thing, while he was at it.

"He's something, isn't he?" said a voice at her shoulder.

"Yes, Mr. Gasparini," Susannah agreed without taking her admiring gaze from the man under discussion, "he is something, all right."

"He could be mayor of this town in a few years. Governor a few years after that. Hell, he could make it all the way to the White House if he put his mind to it."

Susannah turned her head to look at him. "Are you serious?"

"Serious as death and taxes," Harry told her. "Matt's got what it takes to go all the way. The brains, the looks, the record, the family background."

"The desire?" Susannah wondered out loud.

Harry waved her question away. "Public service is a tradition and an obligation in Matt's family," he informed her. "Both his father and grandfather were district court judges. His father made it all the way to the State Supreme Court. His mother's family has an even longer history. There've been Larsons in San Francisco politics since before the Gold Rush. Matt could outshine them all," Harry said. "And he will." He gave Susannah a sidelong glance. "If something, or *somebody*," he added ominously, "doesn't mess it up for him."

"Are you warning me off, Mr. Gasparini?"

Harry shrugged noncommittally. "Let's just say I hope you don't change your mind about marrying him."

"NOW, WAS THAT so bad?" Matt asked a few hours later as he and Susannah walked back to the car, hand in hand once again. The Fourth of July picnic was over, the sack races run, the campaign speeches made, the flesh pressed, the barbecued chicken and potato salad reduced to bones and smears of grease on a paper plate.

"It was kind of fun, actually," Susannah admitted, turning her head to smile up at him. "Especially watching you oh-so-diplomatically poke holes in some of Councilman Leeland's more asinine arguments."

"Which I wouldn't have had to do if you hadn't started those arguments in the first place."

"I didn't start them," Susannah said mildly. "I just sort of—" she grinned mischievously "—helped them along a little."

Matt grinned back at her. "Harry said you were a rabble-rouser."

"Harry did?" *That figures,* she thought. "When?"

"When you were tearing into that man about a woman's right to choose, I think. Or maybe it was when you were showing the Wong twins how to cheat at croquet."

"Smacking your opponent's ball into the bushes is not cheating," she said, letting go of his hand to punch him in the arm. "It's strategy. Those two little girls were being way too polite to win at croquet. The game's all-out war."

"Rabble-rouser," he said, and reached for her hand again.

Then walked on quietly for a moment. Companionably. Content to be walking together through Golden Gate Park in the late afternoon sunshine, with a whole evening of togetherness still ahead of them. They'd been invited to join Carly Elliott on his Sausalito houseboat for a seafood dinner and a front-row seat to watch the fireworks. Matt's mother would be there, too; she and

Carly had seen quite a bit of each other in the two weeks since the fund-raiser at the Mark Hopkins.

"Harry thinks you could be president," Susannah said quietly, looking up at Matt from under her lashes to see how he reacted to her statement.

He seemed unconcerned. "President of what?"

"The United States."

Matt stopped in his tracks and looked down at her, stupefied. He opened his mouth as if to say something, then closed it and shook his head as if he couldn't believe what he'd heard. "You must have misunderstood him."

"Nope," Susannah said. "He said you could make it all the way to the White House if you wanted to."

"He was teasing you."

"'Serious as death and taxes,'" she quoted.

"Well, hell." Matt shook his head again. "I guess I'm going to have to sit down and talk to Harry about his plans for my political future," he said. "President is the last thing in the world I'd ever want to be."

"How about mayor of San Francisco, or governor of the great state of California?"

"Governor, huh?" Matt said consideringly. And then he shook his head, as if dismissing the idea, but Susannah was very much afraid she'd seen what might have been a gleam of interest in his eyes.

THEY LEFT MATT'S CAR in one of the public parking lots at Fisherman's Wharf and caught the ferry over to Sausalito. It docked right in the heart of the little upscale hillside community, letting them disembark less than three blocks from the boat slip Carly Elliott called home.

"I can't believe my mother's dating someone who lives on a houseboat," Matt groused as they strolled along Bridgeway Boulevard. "I mean, why a houseboat? It isn't as if he can't afford a decent place to live." From what he'd learned about him, Matt knew Carlisle Elliott was rich enough to buy several decent places to live; the little nursery business he'd sold before he left Iowa had been a *chain* of nurseries all through the Midwest. "He drives a red Corvette, too," Matt said. "Did I mention that?"

"I think you might have," Susannah said dryly. "Once or twice."

"He took her dancing last Friday at the Pier 23 Café." Friday night was mambo night at Pier 23. "And she said something about catching the midnight show at some club last Tuesday to listen to blues." He snorted. "I didn't even know she knew what the blues were. Yesterday they went kite flying at Ocean Beach." He shook his head morosely. "Kite flying! At their ages," he said, pretending a shock that, at its core, was only half-feigned.

"Lighten up," Susannah advised heartlessly as they stepped onto the wooden pier. "She's having fun. You wanted her to have fun, didn't you?"

Matt shrugged and made a noncommittal noise. *Fun* wasn't a word he ordinarily associated with his mother. Not the kind of fun, anyway, that had her riding around in a red Corvette and kept her out until all hours of the night. His mother was more dignified than that. More conservative. More . . . motherly.

Susannah nudged him with her elbow. "Smile," she said, lifting her hand to return the enthusiastic greeting being directed at them from the top deck of the houseboat docked at the very end of the pier.

"Welcome aboard," Carly called when they got within hollering distance. "Welcome aboard. It's unlocked," he said, pointing at the gate that separated the pier from his gangplank before he disappeared from view.

He reappeared a moment later on the lower deck, looking suntanned and windblown. His sockless feet were encased in a pair of white Topsiders and he wore a flowered Hawaiian print shirt tucked into the waistband of a pair of elegantly rumpled chinos. With his shock of thick, snow-white hair, wide smile and courtly manner, Susannah thought he looked like a retired movie star.

Matt thought he looked like an aging gigolo.

"Millicent will be out in a minute," he told them, gallantly holding out his hand to assist Susannah as she stepped off the gangplank onto the deck. "She went inside to wash up," he explained. "We were doing a little gardening."

"Gardening?" Matt said as he politely extended his hand in greeting. "On a houseboat?"

"I grow herbs and roses in planters on the upper deck. Your mother was helping me with some, ah—" their hands fell apart "—repotting."

"Matthew." Millicent hurried toward them, coming out of a door in the forward cabin. She held her hand out to her son, taking the one he extended to her in turn, and lifted her cheek for his kiss.

Her cheeks were flushed, Matt noticed, her skin warm beneath his lips. Her hair was caught up in a casual ponytail, held in place with a red silk scarf tied into a floppy bow. Her sweater was red, too, the vaguely nautical style accented with two narrow white stripes around the cuff of each sleeve and one outlining the modest V neck.

"And Susannah. How lovely to see you again, dear." She leaned over to kiss Susannah's cheek.

"Lovely to see you again, too," Susannah replied.

"Well, come along, both of you," Millicent said. "Everyone upstairs. Your timing couldn't be better," she told them, talking over her shoulder as she led the way up the narrow wooden staircase to the upper deck. "Carly just whipped up another pitcher of his famous margaritas not ten minutes ago." She looked past Matt and Susannah to smile at the debonair white-haired man who followed behind them. "Didn't you, Carly?"

"Millicent loves my margaritas," Carly said with a grin.

Margaritas? Matt thought. *Another* pitcher of margaritas? Since when had his mother started drinking anything other than Spanish sherry? And when had she started wearing such bright colors? And nail polish? When had she started painting her toe—

And then he saw the dirty handprint smeared across the back of his mother's otherwise immaculate white slacks. It was the kind of smear one might get by absently wiping one's dirty hand across the seat of one's pants. Except that his fastidiously groomed mother was never that careless with her clothes. And her hands weren't nearly that big.

A COUPLE OF HOURS LATER, after margaritas on the upper deck and a light supper of grilled swordfish and green salad, Matt folded his arms across his wide chest and leaned back against the kitchen counter, watching his mother slice into a cherry pie Carly Elliott had made for dessert.

"You've been seeing an awful lot of Elliott these past couple of weeks," he commented, trying to sound casual.

Millicent smiled to herself. "That was the idea, wasn't it?" she said lightly.

"The idea?"

"The idea behind hiring Susannah to find me a date."

Matt wondered why he was even surprised. "You knew?"

Millicent nodded complacently.

"How?"

His mother smiled mysteriously. "A mother always knows."

Matt pursed his lips and cocked an eyebrow at her.

"You made a special point of introducing me to three different men in one week," she said. "It made me wonder. And then someone—I forget who—happened to mention what Susannah really does for a living."

"Ah . . ." Matt nodded.

"Yes," Millicent agreed. She began putting slices of pie on individual plates. "Once I knew that, it wasn't very hard to put two and two together."

"Why didn't you say something?"

"I might have, if it had gone on any longer." Her smile was impish. "Or if you'd introduced me to one more of those excruciatingly boring gentlemen." She opened a drawer for forks, unconsciously revealing her familiarity with Carlisle Elliott's kitchen. "But then Susannah came up with Carly...." She shrugged, saying more by what she didn't say.

"You like him a lot, don't you?"

"Yes," Millicent said. "I do." She looked up at her tall son. "I hope that doesn't upset you."

"He's very different from Dad."

"Yes."

"You're very different with him than you were with Dad."

Millicent sighed. "I loved your father very much, Matthew. I hope you know that."

Matt nodded. "I know."

"For thirty-seven years he was everything to me. Everything I was, everything I did, nearly every aspect of my life revolved around your father and his career. I'm not saying I resented it," she assured her son. "I don't want you to think that. It was the life I'd been raised for, trained for. It was what I wanted and expected when I married your father. But there's a price for building your life around someone else's dream, and when he died, I was totally lost. I felt cast adrift. For a long time it seemed as if I had no purpose anymore." She reached out and put her hand on her son's arm. "Do you understand what I'm saying?"

Matt covered her slender fingers with his and squeezed gently. He could feel her wedding ring pressing against his palm. "I think so."

"I was angry, too," she admitted. "Absolutely furious for a while. I blamed him for dying, for working himself to death, for never taking a vacation or letting up. For leaving me alone." She sighed. "But I got over that, too, and, after a while, when the worst of the grief passed, I started to think my purpose would be you and your career. But I was wrong." She squeezed his arm and let go. "I knew that even before you started trying to arrange those blind dates for me," she said with a smile.

"So, what you're saying is that Elliott gives purpose to your life now."

"No." Millicent looked mildly shocked. "Oh, no, that's not what I'm saying at all! I'm not looking for anyone to give purpose to my life. I've realized that I'm the only one who can do that. But Carly..." She shook her head and grinned. "Carly is a wonderful play-mate."

"A playmate?" Matt said, trying not to sound shocked in turn.

"He's so free and open. So alive to new ideas and new experiences. When I'm with him, I'm a freer person, too. He's teaching me how to have fun," Millicent said, matter-of-factly, "to stop and smell the roses. I've never done that before."

"You're not serious about him, then?"

"Serious?" Millicent shrugged, then shook her head. "I don't know yet." She opened a cupboard and got out a tray. "It might turn into something lasting and, then again, it might not," she said. "For once in my life, I'm not worrying about it either way."

Matt was silent a moment, trying to absorb this new side of his mother, trying to see her as a vibrant, vital woman with needs. "You're being careful, aren't you?"

"Careful?" Millicent said absently, busy arranging the pie plates and cutlery on the tray.

"With, ah . . ." His wide shoulders lifted in an uncomfortable shrug. "Sex and everything?"

Millicent's head snapped around, her hand arrested in midmotion as she reached for the napkins. "Matthew Francis Larson Ryan, are you asking me if I'm sleeping with Carly?"

"No. No, of course not." Matt could feel a blush warming his cheeks. "I was just asking . . . that is . . ." *God, how did I get myself into this conversation?* "I hope you're being careful, that's all."

"If and when I decide to resume a sex life, you can rest assured I'll be very careful," Millicent said, feeling her own cheeks warm. She grabbed a handful of napkins out of the basket on the counter and began folding them. "You can also rest assured that I won't be talking to you about it. As for Carly and me, well, all I'll say about our relationship is what I've already said. Carly's good for me." She slanted a considering look at him out of the corner of her eye as she carefully placed the folded napkins on the dessert tray. "Probably in much the same way that Susannah's good for you," she said delicately, trying to elicit more information from her closemouthed son. "They both have a special gift for livening things up."

Matt gave her a look from under his brows, the previous subject suddenly all but forgotten. "I've asked her to marry me."

Millicent smiled. "I didn't realize it had gone that far already," she said, "but if she's what you want, then I'm happy for both of you."

He reached over and broke a piece of crust off one of the pieces of pie. "Even if she hurts my career?" he asked without looking at her. They both knew his question went deeper than that—that it wasn't just her approval of Susannah he was asking for.

"It's your career, Matthew. Your life. Your choice." She him a level look, rife with unspoken messages. "Don't let anyone or anything else make that choice for you."

MATT AND SUSANNAH STOOD on the upper deck of Carly Elliott's houseboat, shoulders touching, forearms resting on the polished wooden railing, watching the fireworks explode in the ink-black sky over San Francisco Bay. Hand-held sparklers twinkled across the water like fairy lights and, every once in a while, someone shot off an unauthorized rocket or catherine wheel from one of the other boats, sending up a whine and a burst of lights to compete with the official display.

Matt bent his head to whisper in Susannah's ear. "That's the way you make me feel inside," he said as a huge red-white-and-blue chrysanthemum-shaped star burst overhead.

Thrilled beyond words, Susannah turned her head to look at him. They stared at each other for a long moment, their bodies still, barely touching at shoulder and hip, their gazes locked and searching, wrapped in a fog of wonder and romance while the world celebrated all around them.

"I want to feel this way for the rest of my life, Susannah," he whispered, his gaze never leaving hers. "I want you to marry me."

"Oh, Matt." Tears of emotion welled up in her eyes. "Matt. You make me feel like fireworks, too. You make me feel like circuses and birthday parties and Christmas morning all rolled into one, but I—"

He put his fingertip over her lips, stopping her. "That's all I need to hear for now," he said. "We'll talk about the rest of it later."

9

MATT THOUGHT ABOUT stopping by his mother's favorite jeweler before he went to court the next morning but then decided not to. He was already running late as it was. And, alone in a jewelry store, he would probably opt for something traditional, like a simple diamond solitaire. He had a feeling Susannah would want something a bit more original for her engagement ring.

Not that she'd actually given him a *yes* yet; not the unqualified, unequivocal *yes* he wanted from her.

She'd said, "Yes, but we're such different people."

She'd said, "Yes, but let's see how just dating goes first."

She'd said, "Yes, but we really shouldn't rush into it."

She'd said, "Yes, maybe it would work."

She'd said, "Oh, yes, Matt, I love you, too."

Matt was whistling as he entered the courthouse, remembering the passionate circumstances that had engendered her breathy admission and what had come after it. She was his, whether she knew it or not. And he was hers, too. He'd been hers, he realized, since that first crazy, mind-boggling, toe-curling kiss in her office. They were made for each other and, despite politics or life-style or anything else she might come up with, they were destined to be together.

"Matt. Hey, Matt."

Matt slowed, turning to see who had called him, and then stopped. "Cal," he said, holding out his hand in greeting. Cal Westlake had been the man who'd steered him to The Personal Touch in the first place. *Wonder if I should ask him to be best man?* "Cal, how're you doing, buddy?"

"Not nearly as good as you, apparently," Cal said, looking askance at his normally reserved colleague. By tacit agreement, they resumed walking down the long corridor. "I guess you've already seen this morning's *Chronicle?*"

"No, I haven't." He usually skimmed through it over morning coffee after he got to the office, but this particular morning he'd had other things to do. Like make love to Susannah once more before he took her home. He hadn't even been by the office, yet, but had headed directly to the courthouse. "Why?"

"They've endorsed your campaign. I thought that's why you were in such a good mood."

"No, I haven't seen it yet." Unaccountably, his mood dampened a little. "I'll have to pick up a copy during court recess."

"Here." Cal took the folded newspaper out from under his arm and handed it to Matt. "Be my guest."

"Thanks." Matt stopped, motioning toward a set of doors with the folded paper. "This is where I'm headed."

"Catch you back at the office later, then," Cal said and started off down the hall. "Oh—" he stopped and turned back around "—I almost forgot."

Matt paused, his hand already lifted to push open the heavy door. "Forgot what?"

"That dating service I told you about for your mother?" Cal said, walking backward down the hall. "The Personal Touch?"

Matt nodded.

"Seems their touch is real personal, if you know what I mean. I heard through the office grapevine that the place is under investigation."

"Investigation?" Matt echoed.

"Prostitution," Cal said succinctly. "Seems the matchmaker is pimping for teenage runaways on the side."

SUSANNAH SPENT the morning feeling like a manic depressive, frenetically alternating between giddy joy at being loved and in love, and darkest despair because she knew, deep down inside, that, in the long run, nothing would ever come of it. Nothing *could* ever come of it, no matter how they made each other feel.

They were just too different. Strange bedfellows, as she had tried to tell him before.

Matt was a traditionalist; Susannah went out of her way to do things differently.

Matt had wholeheartedly embraced his family's upper-class life-style and values; Susannah had turned her back on hers.

Matt was a middle-of-the road Republican; Susannah was a liberal Democrat.

Matt believed in working within the system; Susannah believed in challenging it at every step.

Matt was a by-the-book lawyer, a prosecutor with the district attorney's office; his job was to put people in jail. When Susannah had worked for the county, her job had been to empathize with the unfortunates she'd been assigned, to find ways to help them out of whatever trouble they were in.

He saw things in black and white, right and wrong; she saw infinite shades of gray and myriad extenuating circumstances.

But what it all boiled down to, really, was that Matt was destined for a brilliant career in politics, and Susannah would never, ever be a proper political wife.

He might try to deny it, to convince her—and himself—that their differences didn't matter, but Susannah knew they did. Harry Gasparini knew it. Councilman Leeland knew it. When it came right down to it, the voters would know it, too.

Oh, she knew it might not matter to Matt right now, not in the beginning when they were still so besotted with each other and anything seemed possible. She strongly suspected he didn't really want to be a district judge, anyway. But if not now, next year or the year after. And if not district judge, then councilman, or state senator, or mayor. His eyes had certainly lit up when she'd spoken the words *governor of California*. And after that, who knew? As Harry had said, Matt had what it took to make it all the way to the White House if he wanted to—but not with her at his side.

"Excuse me, Susannah?"

Susannah looked up from the pad she'd been doodling on, grateful for the interruption. "Yes, Judy?"

"Teri Bowman is here for her interview."

"My goodness," Susannah said, jumping up from her chair. "Is it ten o'clock already?"

"Almost."

Susannah smoothed her hands down the front of her tapestry-brocade vest, tugging on the flared hem to settle it into place over her hips as she came around the desk. She always made it a point to meet her clients in the reception area and escort them into her office. It made them feel more like guests.

"How's computer class going?" she asked pleasantly as Judy stepped back from the door to allow her to exit.

Judy shrugged. "If I don't completely flub the final next week, I'll end up with at least a B + ."

"You'll do fine," Susannah assured her, reaching out to pat Judy's arm. She deliberately kept the gesture brief, quickly taking her hand away to hold it out to her new client. "You must be Teri Bowman," she said with a welcoming smile. "I'm Susannah Bennington."

"Ms. Bennington."

"Susannah, please. We're very informal around here. You've met Helen and Judy, haven't you?" she asked, smiling at her assistants. "Good," she said when the woman nodded. "Then we can get started." She gestured toward her office. "If you'll just step into my office, we can—"

The phone rang, cutting her off.

Both Judy and Helen reached for the receiver.

"The Personal Touch," Helen said as she lifted the receiver to her ear. "How may I help you?"

Susannah hesitated, waiting to see who it was. Even though Matt had said he would be tied up in court all day, she was halfway expecting—hoping—he would call. She hadn't heard his voice in almost three hours.

"Excuse me?" Helen said into the receiver. "Who did you want to speak to?"

Susannah suddenly knew by the older woman's expression that it wasn't Matt on the phone. Helen wouldn't get upset over a phone call from Matt.

"No," Helen said to the caller. "There's no one here by that name. Yes, I'm sure. No, I told you," she said, her voice rising with agitation, "there's no one here by that name." She slammed the phone down.

"Another call for Isabel?" Susannah asked with a grimace. Lately, they'd had a rash of unsavory massage-parlor-type callers asking for a woman named Isabel.

Too agitated to speak, Helen only nodded.

"Since the calls upset you so much," Judy offered, "maybe I should be the only one to answer the phone from now on when I'm here." Her expression hardened. "It takes more than a phone call to shock me."

"No," Helen said. "No, that's all right. I can handle it. It's part of my job, and I can handle it. Really," she said, looking up at Susannah. "I don't need to be protected. I'll be fine."

"All right," Susannah said. "If that's what you want." She turned and smiled at her new client. "Shall we?" she said, gesturing toward the open door of her office. "Before we get started," the two women in the outer office heard her say to Teri Bowman just before she closed the door, "I'd like to explain what that was all about...."

"YOU THINK *WHAT*?" Susannah demanded, staring at Matt from across the width of her desk.

"You heard me. Judy Sukura is up to her old tricks."

"I don't believe it."

"Ask her," he challenged.

"I don't need to ask her," Susannah said reasonably, "because I know she isn't." She shook her head. "She wouldn't."

"Then how do you explain her meetings with Eddie Devine?"

"Meetings with..." Susannah stared at him, aghast. "She wouldn't meet with Eddie. She hates Eddie."

"She's met him twice right outside this building."

"Those weren't meetings. Not the way you're suggesting. Eddie accosted her. He—" She broke off. "How do you know that?"

"It doesn't matter how I know," Matt said, brushing her question aside. The particulars of a case under investigation were never up for discussion outside the DA.'s office until the case went to court. "All that matters is that she was seen meeting him."

"But those weren't meetings. Eddie accosted her on the street when she was coming out of The Tea Cozy."

"How do you know that?"

"I saw them. Both times. I was standing by the window and I saw them."

"Did you also happen to hear what was said?"

"I didn't need to, because Judy told me what was said."

"Which was?"

"That she wouldn't do what he wanted. That he couldn't make her do it."

"'It' being?"

"Well . . ." Susannah hesitated. "Going back to work for him. She didn't say exactly, but I know that's what she meant."

"Hearsay," Matt said coolly. "Inadmissible in a court of law."

"Well, this isn't a court of law," Susannah snapped. "And I'm not on the witness stand," she added indignantly. "And I certainly don't appreciate you firing questions at me as if I were."

"You're right." Matt turned toward the closed door to Susannah's office. "The one who should be answering a few questions is Judy."

"No." Susannah jumped up from her chair. "Don't you dare." She ran around the desk, placing herself between him and the door. "I will not have Judy upset by a lot of unfounded suspicions. Especially not now. She's got finals coming up next week."

"Would you rather have her turning tricks in your office?"

"What a disgusting thing to say! Judy isn't turning tricks in my office or anywhere else."

"You don't know that for a fact."

"I *do* know it for a fact. For heaven's sake, Matt. When would she have the time? She works here all morning. She goes to school in the afternoons and most nights. And the nights she's not in school, she's in therapy."

"Are you sure she actually goes to school? To therapy?"

"Of course I'm sure! They're both conditions of her parole."

"People break parole all the time."

Susannah shook her head in exasperation. "Her teachers would notify her parole officer if she was cutting classes. So would her therapist. Believe me, Matt, Judy isn't turning tricks."

"Maybe not personally," Matt agreed. *Apparently, the matchmaker is pimping for teenage runaways.* "Maybe she's recruited Heather, and other girls like her, to do the dirty work."

Susannah just stared at him, unable to believe what she was hearing. He'd met Judy. He'd met Heather. How could he think either one of them would do what he was suggesting? How could he just believe the worst of them like that? "You're way off base here, Counselor," she said icily. "Judy isn't turning tricks and she hasn't recruited Heather to turn them for her. End of discussion."

"Dammit, Susannah, you can't just bury your head in the sand. There's a reason The Personal Touch is being investigated. And Judy Sukura is part of that rea—"

"Investigated?" Susannah interrupted, shock and incredulity evident in her voice. "The Personal Touch is being investigated?"

Matt bit back a curse. He hadn't meant to tell her that. Strictly speaking, he shouldn't have told her; it was unethical to discuss a case under investigation with anyone outside the DA.'s office, even if you weren't working on it yourself. But maybe it was for the best. Maybe she'd listen to reason if she knew how serious it was.

"The Personal Touch is under investigation as a possible front for prostitution."

Susannah just stared at him, openmouthed with shock.

"I haven't had a chance to check it out thoroughly because I've been in court all day but, according to what I know so far, you and Eddie Devine are suspected of using the dating service as a cover for running a string of underage girls. Runaways, like Heather."

"Do you believe that?"

"No, of course not," Matt said, insulted that she would even think that of him. "Don't be silly. I know you don't have anything to do with it."

"But you think it is going on and you think Judy's involved in it."

"Yes," he said honestly. "I think Judy's involved in it up to her eyebrows."

"And Heather? You think Heather's involved in it, too?"

Matt hesitated, remembering the teasing sway of the girl's hips as she'd preceded him up the stairs, the sexy pout she'd turned on him. *See anything you like?* she'd said. "Maybe," he admitted reluctantly.

"How about Helen?" she said then, goading him. "Is Helen involved?"

"Susannah." He reached out to put his hands on her shoulders. "I know you're upset, but—"

She backed away from him, taking herself out of his reach. "Upset doesn't even begin to cover it," she said with dangerous calm. "I'm incensed. Enraged." She curled her hands into fists. "I'm so mad I could spit.

Dammit—" she blinked furiously, fighting back hot tears of rage "—how *could* you, Matt? How could you believe that garbage about Judy and Heather? How could you believe I'm so stupid I wouldn't know if something like that was going on right under my nose?"

"Not stupid," Matt said gently. "Naive."

"Oh, excuse me. *Naive*," she sneered, her inflection making a curse of the word.

"Now, Susannah," he began placatingly, but she cut him off.

"All it took was just a hint of . . . of—" she groped for a word "—impropriety and everyone's instantly presumed guilty. Without question. Without a doubt in your mind. Guilty as charged."

"Now, wait just a minute, Susannah. I never said you were guilty of anything but—"

"—but being naive. I know." As far as she was concerned, calling her naive was just a polite way of saying she'd been stupid—and she didn't like either word. "I knew it wouldn't work," she said, as much to herself as to him. "Right from the minute we met, I *knew* it. And then I went ahead and let myself get involved, anyway. I let my—" She broke off and turned away from him, blindly reaching out to fiddle with the placement of a glass paperweight on her desk. "I think you'd better go," she said, fighting the urge to hurl it against the wall. "Before one of us says—" *or does* "—something we'll be sorry for."

"This isn't over, Susannah. It isn't something you can just sweep under the rug and ignore, hoping it will go away. It won't go away." He put his hands on her upper arms and turned her around. "And neither will I. So don't think you're going to use this as an excuse to break it off between us."

Susannah kept her head turned away. "Don't you have to be back in court this afternoon?" she said, refusing to look at him.

Matt stood there for a second, holding her in front of him, his hands on her arms, wondering whether to shake some sense into her or kiss her senseless. Either one would have been highly satisfying at that moment. But she was right, he did have to be back in court.

"Susannah." He shook her lightly when she continued to ignore him. "Susannah, look at me."

Grudgingly, she lifted her gaze to his.

"We'll finish this discussion later tonight."

"No, we won't," she said mulishly. "I have a client party tonight. I'll be very busy."

"All right, tomorrow, then," he said with exaggerated patience, as if she were a fractious child. "In the meantime, I don't want you to do or say anything to anybody. Don't talk to Judy or Heather about any of this. And if Eddie Devine should come around again, for God's sake, don't try to confront him. He could be dangerous. Is that clear?"

"Are you speaking as a concerned friend and lover?" she asked snidely. "Or is this an order from an officer of the court?"

Matt wondered which one she'd be more apt to listen to. "As the man who's going to marry you," he said firmly. Then, ignoring her stiffness, he pressed a quick, hard kiss on her mouth before he left.

Susannah threw the paperweight at the closed door and burst into tears.

"I KNOW WE HAD an agreement, Heather," Susannah said. "And I really hate to ask you to do this, but do you think you could help out at the party? Helen went home early with a sick headache, or I wouldn't ask you."

"Can't Judy do it?"

"She'll be here right after her computer class. But since this is our first evening dance party I'd really like to have an extra hand."

"What would I, like, have to do?"

"Nothing too taxing," Susannah assured her. "Greet people at the door and then pass the hors d'oeuvres on a tray. You'll be finished by nine-thirty. Ten at the latest. And I'll pay you five dollars an hour."

The flash of mercenary interest in Heather's eyes was quickly overshadowed by a teenager's instinctive caution. "Like, what's the catch?"

"You have to wear a dress."

"A dress?"

"You can borrow one of mine if you want to."

"Yeah?" Her expression brightened. "Cool. Which one?"

"Any one you want. Within reason."

"Yeah?" Heather said again. And then she tilted her head, eyeing Susannah consideringly. "You all right, Suse?" she asked. "You look a little down, you know?"

"I'm fine," Susannah lied.

But Heather wasn't so easily put off. "Fight with the ambulance chaser, huh?"

Susannah shrugged.

"Helen said she heard you guys 'having words' this afternoon. And there's, like, a dent in the plaster next to your door. What'd you throw at him?"

"A paperweight," Susannah admitted. "But I missed."

"Too bad," Heather commiserated. She hesitated, clearly wanting to say more, also clearly uncomfortable about it.

"What?" Susannah urged.

Heather shrugged. "I, ah, guess this means he's not going to help me with my case, huh?"

"No, of course not," Susannah assured her. "Whatever happens between Matt and me has nothing to do with you. He's already filed a report with the juvenile authorities on your behalf. He isn't going to rescind it just because he and I had a disagreement."

"Yeah?" Heather said hopefully.

Her petition for emancipated-minor status was vitally important to her, no matter how hard she pretended it wasn't. She'd started running away from home when she was twelve, when her father's physical abuse—and her mother's downtrodden acceptance of it—had finally became too much for her to handle. Each time she'd been returned by the juvenile authorities until the last time, when she'd threatened to kill herself if they made her go back. She now faced living in an institutional environment or with a foster family until she turned eighteen. But she'd been on her own too long to easily accept someone else's authority, even for two years. She'd been about to run away again when Susannah told her about the possibility of becoming an emancipated minor. The chance that it might actually come to pass was the only thing that kept Heather from disappearing into the streets again.

Susannah crossed the room and took Heather's face in her hands. "I promise you," she said. "No matter what happens between me and Matt, he'll do everything he can for you."

She hoped like hell she'd just spoken the truth.

AT SEVEN-THIRTY that evening everything was ready for the party. The champagne was cooling in a small silver tub on the sideboard. The hors d'oeuvres were temptingly arranged on silver trays. Vintage Frank Sinatra alternated with Tony Bennett on the music system. And Heather Lloyd was wearing a dress.

It was one of Susannah's simpler dresses: a short-sleeved, scoop-necked French challis with tiny ivory flowers scattered over a chocolate-brown background. A row of tiny pearlescent buttons ran from the neckline to the ballet-length hem. Heather wore them undone to midthigh with ivory leggings underneath to save her from immodesty and her heavy black boots to preserve her independence. She'd left the pentagrams and crosses off her ears without being asked, replacing them with small delicate studs also of her own design.

"You look charming," Susannah said, meaning it sincerely. Heather was young and pretty enough to look charming in practically anything she wore.

"And you look really hot," Heather replied, eyeing Susannah's long purple dress with undisguised approval.

It was perfectly plain and perfectly fitted, long-sleeved and slightly off the shoulder, with a touch of Lycra to make it cling to every slender curve from shoulder to midcalf. Her ankle-strap high heels and sheer panty hose matched it exactly, creating a long, unbroken line of color. A pair of crystal drop earrings Heather had made for her and her wild red hair were her only accessories.

"Are you, like, expecting the ambulance chaser, Suse?"

Susannah shrugged. "No," she said. *But it never hurts to be prepared, just in case.* "I just had the urge to dress up a little tonight. It always makes me feel better when I'm depressed."

"You still, like, upset about the fight you guys had?"

Susannah shrugged again and went to answer the front door.

By eight o'clock the party was in full swing. The champagne was flowing. The hors d'oeuvres were fast disappearing. The mellow, crooning voice of Frank Sinatra had been replaced by Big Band dance tunes. And a spry gentleman of seventy-one was teaching Heather the swing step.

Judy arrived at eight-forty-five, dressed in her usual unrelieved, sophisticated black.

"How's it going?" she asked Susannah as she stowed her schoolbooks in the kitchen and donned a ruffled white apron.

"Even better than I'd hoped," Susannah said, giving her a hand as they replenished the hors d'oeuvres trays. "Teri Bowman and Harold Whitley are hitting it off, just as I thought they would. And Sarah Moore has had *two* invitations to dinner already." She smiled brightly, pleased with the success of her idea. "I knew she'd be a hit with the fellas if I could just get her to loosen up a little."

"Looks like Heather's a real hit, too," Judy commented with a wry smile.

Susannah laughed softly. "I know. You could have knocked me over with a feather. I didn't expect her to be quite so enthusiastic about helping out. But she's been a big help."

"Well," Judy said, picking up the refurbished platter of hors d'oeuvres, "it looks like the party's a success, then," she said over her shoulder as she left the kitchen.

"A big success," Susannah echoed, wondering why she wasn't more elated.

But she knew why. The party might be a rousing success but what good was that if her business got closed down on some trumped-up prostitution charge?

Or, maybe, she admitted to herself as she watched Judy move among the guests with her silver tray—just maybe—the charges weren't trumped up at all. When the party was over and all the guests were gone, she was going to have to force herself to ask some hard questions.

AT NINE O'CLOCK the doorbell rang.

"Heather, would you get that, please," Susannah called over her shoulder, busy refilling champagne glasses for her guests after a particularly strenuous cha-cha had rendered them all in need of refreshment.

"Sure thing, Suse," Heather said, disappearing through the arched doors into the foyer. She was back a second later. "Ah, Suse?" she said, sticking her head around the edge of the parlor door. "Could you com'ere a minute?"

"Who is it?"

"I really think you, like, need to come out here."

Still holding the champagne bottle in one hand, Susannah headed for the door. "Yes?" she said, smiling at the man standing in the doorway.

He flashed a badge at her. "Ms. Susannah Bennington?"

"Yes?" Susannah said, the beginnings of alarm snaking up her spine. "What is it? Is someone hurt?"

"No, ma'am." He slipped the badge back into his coat pocket and produced a folded sheet of paper, all in one smooth move. He unfurled the paper with a practiced snap of his wrist. "I have a warrant to search the premises, ma'am."

"A search warrant?" Susannah echoed. "Why?"

"Vice." He stepped inside, beckoning behind him for his backup. Half a dozen uniformed officers suddenly swarmed into the room. "You and everybody in the house are under arrest."

10

THE RINGING TELEPHONE woke Matt from an uneasy sleep, one disturbed by too many cups of reheated coffee, too much printed legalese and frustrating, arousing, elusive dreams of a slender, red-haired woman who ran ahead of him in a circus parade, always just out of reach. He rolled to a sitting position on the sofa, sending the case file he'd been reading sliding to the floor, and groped for the cellular phone. In his hasty search, he knocked a pile of folders off the coffee table and onto the carpet, before finally wrapping his fingers around the instrument. He stabbed at the *Talk* button three times before the red light came on and the ringing stopped.

"What?" he barked into the receiver, more than ready to take his bad mood out on whoever had been unwise enough to make him or herself available.

"Matthew?"

"Mom?" Matt rubbed a hand up over his face and through his hair. "What is it?"

"I think you'd better turn on the television, Matthew," his mother said, her soft, even tones failing to hide the note of anxiety in her voice.

"The television?"

"Channel Two," she said. "The eleven o'clock news report."

Without taking the phone from his ear, Matt reached for the remote control and aimed it at the television. He punched it on. Two clicks brought him to the proper channel.

"Former San Francisco debutante, Susannah Bennington, owner of The Personal Touch dating service, is being held in connection with an alleged prostitution ring involving female minors. She was arrested at her Pacific Heights home earlier this evening. Two of her employees, convicted prostitute Judy Sukura and an unnamed minor female, were arrested with her. Several of her alleged customers were also taken into custody at the same location, where a wild party was in progress at the time of the arrests. We take you now, live, to the scene."

Matt sat bolt upright on the sofa. "Good God!" he breathed as the scene shifted from the newsroom to the street outside of Susannah's house.

"Behind me, in this quiet Victorian house, in this pleasant, well-to-do section of the city, an alleged prostitution ring has been operating under the guise of a genteel dating service. The owner of this dating service, Susannah Bennington, is the daughter of Roger Bennington, founder and owner of Bennington Plastics, and Audrey Stanhope Bennington Harper, one of our city's most active civic leaders. Neighbors say that Ms. Bennington has always been 'a little different' and often had 'strange characters' going in and out of her establishment...."

"But I never thought much of it," said another talking head, obviously the aforementioned neighbor. "San Francisco has a lot of strange people in it."

The on-location reporter signed off, the scene shifted to the outside of the police station and the news anchor began to give a description of the scene—but Matt wasn't listening.

He watched, shocked and disbelieving, as Susannah was helped from the back seat of a police car. She was wearing a slinky, shoulder-baring dress, spike heels and a pair of stainless-steel handcuffs. Her hair was wild, half falling in her face, giving her a wanton look. Her chin was well up, her carriage as haughty as a queen's despite the handcuffs. Her face was set in stubborn, unyielding lines, two spots of color flaming high on her cheekbones. Her brown eyes were huge in her pale face, wide and frightened despite her brave front.

Judy Sukura slid out of the back seat after her, wearing some kind of sexy maid's uniform. Beneath the sleek, sophisticated hairstyle and expertly applied makeup, her face was expressionless and cold, making her look as hard as nails.

In contrast, the "unknown minor female" being helped out of a second police car looked even younger than the sixteen Matt knew her to be. Her green eyes were defiant, her mouth was sulky, her slender shoulders were hunched in a way Matt already recognized as defensive and self-protective. The position caused the front of her pretty flowered dress to gape, exposing more of her chest to the cameras than it should have, and managing to make her look sexy and innocent at the same time.

"Matthew, are you there?"

"Yes, Mom," he said, his gaze glued to the television screen. "I'm here."

"Do you know what this is all about?"

"Not really," he hedged, automatically shielding what he knew of the facts. Despite his lapse this afternoon with Susannah, it was his usual procedure; a case under investigation wasn't supposed to be discussed until the investigation was complete. Apparently, this investigation was more complete than he'd thought, since they were already making arrests.

He wondered if they'd picked up Eddie Devine, too. And why the cameras weren't fighting for close-ups of him. Probably because the little slimeball wasn't nearly as photogenic as the women.

"According to a reliable source, the high-society madam has friends in high places. She was recently seen in the company of Assistant District Attorney Matthew Ryan at a campaign fund-raiser at the Mark Hopkins hotel. Ryan, son of the late State Supreme Court Justice, Francis Ryan, is currently running for district judge."

"I've got to go, Mom. I've got to get down there."

"Sources at Ryan's campaign headquarters denied there was any relationship between the candidate and Ms. Bennington," the reporter intoned importantly as the scene continued to unfold.

Harry Gasparini's face suddenly filled the screen.

"Susannah Bennington was a guest at the fund-raiser," he said easily, standing in front of a Matthew Ryan for District Judge banner. "She purchased a ticket, just like hundreds of other people. I believe she and

Matt Ryan sat at the same table with seven or eight other people during dinner. But the suggestion that they have any kind of a close or intimate relationship is completely unfounded."

"I'll talk to you later, Mom," Matt said, severing the phone connection. Swearing viciously, he got to his feet, yanked his trench coat from the brass coatrack by the front door, and stormed out into the night like an avenging angel hell-bent on destruction and rescue.

The television continued broadcasting to an empty room.

"I TOLD YOU," Susannah said to the police detective for what seemed like at least the hundredth time. "I don't have any idea what you're talking about. The Personal Touch is not a front for prostitution. I am not some kind of madam. I was not having some kind of lurid sex party. My God, have you looked at my guests? Most of them are over sixty!"

"But you don't deny that Judy Sukura works for you?"

"No, I don't deny it. Why would I deny it when I've already admitted it?" Susannah said in exasperation. "Judy Sukura is my part-time receptionist."

"And Heather Lloyd? What does she do for you?"

"Heather doesn't *do* anything for me. She's a house-guest. She's been living at my home for a little over two months."

"Do you often have young female minors living with you?"

"I have a small bed-sitting room on the lower floor of my house. It's frequently occupied by someone who needs a safe place to stay."

"And is attending your parties one of the requirements of living in that room?"

"No, it is not," Susannah said evenly, telling herself not to let his insinuations rattle her. That's just what he was trying to do.

"Then what was Ms. Lloyd doing at that party tonight?"

"A favor."

"Does she do these kinds of 'favors' often?"

Susannah glared at him.

The detective didn't appear to be intimidated. "Does she, Ms. Bennington?" he repeated.

"No," Susannah said wearily. "She doesn't. This is the first time I've asked her to help out."

"And why is that?"

"Because my regular assistant had to go home early."

"That would be—" he glanced down at his notes as if he needed to refresh his memory "—Helen Sanford?"

"Yes."

"And Ms. Sanford went home early because?"

"She wasn't feeling well."

"Exactly what time did she go home?"

"About two o'clock. Maybe two-thirty. I don't remember exactly." It had been some time after Matt had left her office after their argument and she'd been too upset to pay much attention to the clock.

The detective took a sip of coffee from a paper cup. "What's your relationship with Eddie Devine?"

"I told you, I don't have a relationship with Eddie Devine."

"Who's Isabel?"

"I don't know any Isabel," Susannah said through clenched teeth. "I already told you that, too."

"Tell me again."

"Dammit!" Susannah exploded. Coming to her feet, she slammed her hand down on the table. "I just did!"

The detective was unimpressed. "Sit down, Ms. Bennington."

"I'm tired of sitting down," Susannah replied. "I'm tired of answering your ridiculous accusations. Most of all, I'm tired of you."

She looked at the woman who was sitting quietly in the seat beside the one she'd just vacated. She was a friend dating back to Susannah's days as a social worker. When the police detective had asked her if she wanted a lawyer present, Carole's was the only name she could think of, besides the one that came instantly to mind—and was just as instantly rejected. She couldn't call Matt.

"How much longer do I have to put up with this?" she asked her lawyer.

"Until I'm satisfied with your answers," said the detective.

"Carole?" Susannah said to the lawyer.

"You can refuse to continue this conversation at any time," Carole advised her.

"And then?"

"And then we lock you up," the detective said.

"How long can they keep me in jail?"

"Until tomorrow morning, at least. That's when you'll go before a judge for arraignment. Given your long-standing ties to the community, I can probably get you released on your own recognizance."

"What about the others? Judy and Heather and my guests?"

Carole shook her head. "Given Judy Sukura's record and the nature of the charges, her bail is likely to be fairly high."

"I'll take care of it," Susannah said. "What about Heather?"

"She's already been turned over to the juvenile authorities. They'll notify her family and appoint a lawyer for her if she doesn't already have one."

Susannah closed her eyes for a moment. Heather would hate having her family notified. She'd be afraid, too, although she'd never admit it. "Will they turn her over to her parents?"

"Legally, she can be remanded to their custody. But I don't think that will happen, not given the history of abuse. They'll probably keep her in custody at juvie."

Susannah relaxed a little, knowing that, for now, Heather was safe. Probably mad as a wet hen, but safe.

"Can we get back to the subject here, ladies?" the detective said.

Susannah ignored him. "And my guests? What will happen to them?"

"They're being released as soon as they've given their statements," Carole told her. "Most of them are already gone."

"Ladies?"

Wearily, Susannah sat down.

"What's your relationship with Eddie Devine?"

"I don't have a relationship with Eddie Devine."

"Isn't he Judy Sukura's pimp?"

"He *was* Judy's pimp. He isn't anymore."

"Who's Isa—"

A knock sounded on the interrogation-room door. "Excuse me. Detective Martin, can I see you out here a minute?"

Without a word, the detective got up and left the room.

Susannah looked at her lawyer. "What's going to happen?"

"It's hard to say. I haven't seen the evidence against you yet, so—"

"There isn't any evidence," Susannah said, "because I haven't done anything."

"You haven't," Carole agreed. "But what about Judy?"

"She wouldn't." Susannah prayed it was true. "I know she wouldn't."

"Judy has a record going back seven years. She's a prostitute."

"*Was* a prostitute."

"Maybe," Carole said. "And maybe not. You have to face facts, Susannah. Judy might be guilty."

"How could she be? I mean, it's ridiculous if you just think about it for a minute. How could she possibly be running a prostitution ring from The Personal Touch, with or without Eddie Devine's help? Helen answers the phone as often as Judy does. More often, because she's there more hours. I answer it, too. Even Heather has answered it," she added, remembering that afternoon in her office a few weeks ago when she'd found Heather on the phone. With a friend, she'd said. "So tell me, how could Judy be running some kind of prostitution ring right under our noses and none of us know it?"

"Maybe she's not doing it alone. Have you thought of that? Maybe Heather *is* involved somehow. As far as we know, the trouble didn't start until after she came to live with you. She might very well be involved."

"No," Susannah said. "I refuse to believe Heather would—" The door to the interrogation room opened. Susannah's eyes widened in shock. "Matt."

"Susannah. For God's sake!" In three strides, Matt was across the room and hauling Susannah out of her chair by the shoulders. He crushed her to him. "Are you all right?"

Susannah clung to him for a moment, her eyes closed in silent thanksgiving. She'd never been so glad to see anyone in her entire life.

"Susannah?"

"Matt," she said into his chest. Her fingers were curled into the lapels of his trench coat, her knuckles white from the strength of her grip. "Matt."

He lifted one hand to her face, turning it up to his. "Are you all right?" he demanded, tenderly brushing back her hair so he could look into her eyes.

She nodded against his palm, too near tears to trust her voice just then.

"They didn't hurt you?" He slid his hands down her arms, gently pulling her hands from his lapels so he could examine the delicate skin of her wrists.

"She hasn't got a single bruise on her lily-white skin," the detective said, his tone sardonic. "We hadn't got around to the rubber hoses yet."

Matt ignored him and enfolded Susannah in his arms once again. "Dammit," he said into her hair. "Why in hell didn't you call me?"

"You shouldn't be here," she said, trying to pull herself out of his arms. "Your campaign. The press. They were all over the place when the police brought us in." She glanced nervously at the detective who was leaning back against the wall with his arms folded, watching them with obvious interest. "You shouldn't be here, Matt."

Matt refused to let her go. "You should have called me," he reiterated firmly. "I should have been the first person you called."

Susannah deliberately misunderstood. "I have a lawyer," she said. "Carole's my lawyer."

Matt looked at the other woman over Susannah's head. "With all due respect, Counselor," he said. "I'll be taking over this case from here."

"Susannah?" Carole said, looking to her client for direction.

Susannah lifted her gaze to Matt's. "You know what this will do to your campaign, don't you?" she whispered.

Matt smiled tenderly, touched by her concern for him in the face of her own problems. "I have a fairly good idea."

"There's nothing linking us yet in the public mind. There've been no stories about us in the papers yet. No gossip. If you leave now, there probably won't be."

"Sweetheart, there already is. Some 'reliable source' reported having seen us together at the Mark Hopkins."

Susannah's eyes widened. "In the coatroom?"

"At dinner."

"Then it's still all right," she breathed, relieved. "You can make some kind of statement about how I was just there to make a campaign contribution."

"A bleeding-heart liberal contributing to my campaign?" He shook his head. "The press'll never buy it. Besides, someone from the Fourth of July picnic is bound to come forward. No matter what I do tonight, by tomorrow morning we'll be the lead story in both papers."

Susannah closed her eyes. "I'm sorry, Matt."

"Don't be." He leaned down and kissed her lightly. "I'm not."

"This is all very touching, folks," the police detective said then, still watching them from his position

against the wall, "but I have an interrogation to conduct here."

Matt shifted his hold on Susannah, bringing her
around to his side with his arm curled protectively
around her shoulders. "The interrogation is over," he
said. "I'm taking her out of here."

The police detective straightened away from the wall.

Matt stopped him with a look. "I've already cleared
it with your lieutenant, Detective Martin. Ms. Bennington has been released to my custody until this mess
is cleared up."

"Does that mean I'm fired?" Carole asked.

Susannah looked up at Matt, silently offering him
one last chance to do the sensible thing.

"I'm not leaving here without you," he said.

"What about Judy? And Heather? I can't leave them
here."

"And if they're guilty?"

"I still can't leave them here."

Matt nodded. "All right. I'll see what I can do about
getting them released, too."

Susannah looked over at Carole with an apologetic
smile. "I'm sorry, you're fired," she said.

MATT POKED HIS HEAD into the interrogation room.
"You two ready to go?" he asked, looking back and
forth between the two women sitting at the table.

Judy pushed her cup of coffee away and stood up.
"I'm more than ready," she said fervently, although her
face was devoid of all emotion. Whether she was upset

or not, frightened or not, was anybody's guess. Matt assumed she'd had a lot of practice hiding what she was feeling.

Susannah, on the other hand, was an open book. Every emotion she was feeling showed in her expressive face. She was angry, frightened and determined. She was also shivering.

"Here, put this on," Matt said, shrugging out of his trench coat to wrap it around her bare shoulders. "It's colder outside than it is in here."

"Did you get Heather released?" Susannah asked as she slipped her arms into the coat sleeves.

Matt nodded. "I had to pull in a few favors, and promise a few more, but I got the juvenile authorities to release her to my custody. Carole went over to pick her up." Matt put his arm around Susannah's shoulders and slipped a hand under Judy's elbow, leading them toward the door as he spoke. "She'll meet us over at my mother's."

Susannah stopped dead. "Your mother's?"

"I can't take you back to your place, or mine, for that matter. Not right now. The reporters will be waiting for us."

"I don't mind a few reporters," Judy said, slipping her arm out of his hand. "I can get myself home."

"I'm sure you can," Matt said, reaching out to recapture it. "But you're coming with us. I plan to conduct a little interrogation of my own." His expression hardened into one any hostile witness he'd ever questioned would have recognized. "Before the night's over, I'm going to get to the bottom of this." He started toward the door again, a woman held firmly in either hand. "When we get outside," he warned, "don't say anything to anyone. Not even 'no comment.' Is that clear?"

Both women nodded.

"If any talking needs to be done, I'll do it." He paused, looking from one woman to the other. "Ready? Okay, here we go."

It was pandemonium outside the police station. They were instantly surrounded by reporters thrusting microphones and minicams in their faces.

"Mr. Ryan, what's your relationship to the High Society Madam?"

"Are you and Ms. Bennington lovers?"

"What does this mean to your campaign?"

"Ms. Bennington, were your parents aware of what you do for a living before tonight?"

"Are the rumors about young girls being coerced into providing sexual favors for elderly clients true?"

"Are you going to pull out of the campaign now?"

Silently, slowly, stoically, they made their way to the car parked at the curb, ignoring the noise and confusion swirling around them. Matt opened the front passenger door and assisted Susannah inside. Judy pulled open the back door and quickly climbed in, locking the door after her.

"Mr. Ryan, were you aware that Ms. Bennington was a prostitute before you became involved with her?"

Matt's head jerked around. He leveled a killing glance at the man who had asked the question. "My *fiancée*—" he placed a subtle but unmistakable emphasis on the word "—and I will have a statement for the press in the morning."

11

MATT LOOKED AROUND the circle of feminine faces
staring back at him from their seats in his mother's front
parlor. Heather, Judy, his mother and Susannah returned his gaze with varying degrees of seriousness and
concern.

"The way I see it," he said, "we're left with only one
possible alternative."

Susannah shook her head, but she wasn't really dis-
agreeing with what he'd said. She couldn't see any other
answer, either. "I can hardly believe it," she said, half
to herself.

"Just examine what we know so far," Matt said. "For
the last few weeks, at least, Eddie Devine has been using The Personal Touch to set up appointments for
some of his girls. That means he has to have someone
on the inside. You weren't doing it," he said to Susannah. "Judy and Heather swear they didn't have anything to do with it, either."

"And I believe them," Susannah interjected, smiling
at each of the younger women in turn. "Completely."

"As do I," Matt agreed. *Now.* "So that leaves only
one possible suspect."

"Wow," said Heather, speaking for all of them. "Who
would'a, like, thought *Helen* would do something like
this in a million years?"

"When you think about it logically," Matt said, "it really couldn't be anyone else. The key is the telephone. Helen answers it more than the rest of you put together. When the voice on the other end asked for Isabel, *she* knew what that meant. That it was a code word. When one of you answered it, you just assumed it was a wrong number and hung up. You told me yourself, Susannah, that you've gotten calls like that on a more-or-less regular basis ever since you opened for business. Helen had to be hoping you'd just think these were more of the same."

"But Helen was upset by those calls," Susannah said. "Remember, Judy? That other afternoon when we got one? Teri Bowman had just come in for her appointment and the phone rang. Remember?" She looked back at Matt. "Helen was very upset by it."

"Of course she would be upset," Matt said patiently. "If you and Judy were standing in the room when the call came, how could she not be upset? You might have tumbled onto what was going on."

"I still can't believe...." She shook her head. "How could she have thought it would have worked? Surely she must have known.... She *had* to realize we'd become suspicious sooner or later."

"Ah, but would you have?" Matt asked. "Think about it. If it hadn't been for the ongoing investigation into Eddie Devine's activities and the subsequent raid on your place, would you have suspected? Or would you just have gone on assuming someone had given out a wrong number?"

Susannah shrugged, tacitly admitting the truth of his assessment.

"What I don't, like, understand," said Heather, "is how Eddie thought this whole thing would work, anyway. I mean, like, when Susannah or Judy got calls for this Isabel, they just hung up. Wouldn't that kinda, like, you know, make his customers mad? Or make 'em dial up some other escort service? I don't see how this Eddie character thought he could, like, stay in business that way, you know?"

"Eddie's stupid," Judy told her, her soft mouth flat with distaste. "He's mean and vicious, but he's stupid. He saw what he thought was a golden opportunity and he took it."

Matt nodded, agreeing with her assessment. "A task force has been shadowing Eddie for the past two months. Until recently he just ran street girls, young but not young enough to gain him any special attention from the authorities. He got that when he started adding minors to his string. That was his first mistake. His second was in thinking he could use The Personal Touch to upgrade his dirty little operation."

"Upgrade?" Millicent said.

"Call girls get more money for their services than streetwalkers," Judy said flatly. "And the younger they are, the more expensive they are."

"How long has he been setting up appointments through The Personal Touch?" Susannah wanted to know.

"Not long," Matt assured her. "Maybe two weeks at the most." His smile was Machiavellian in its satisfaction. "As Judy said, he's stupid. So stupid that he didn't think any of it through. There was no way in hell it could have worked. Even if the department hadn't already been investigating him, it wouldn't have worked. The logistics and the infrastructure just weren't there."

"There's still something I don't completely understand about all of this," Millicent said.

They all looked at her.

"Why would he want to use the phone lines at The Personal Touch in the first place? Wouldn't it have been easier to set up his own?"

"You'd think so," Matt said. "But that's where Eddie's lack of intelligence comes into play. He thought using The Personal Touch would save him the trouble and expense of setting up his own operation."

"But—"

"Eddie thinks everyone else is as greedy and stupid as he is, Mrs. Ryan," Judy said. "Especially women. He probably didn't think any of us would even notice anything was going on."

"But *Helen*," Heather insisted. "How'd he, like, get *Helen* to help him? She pretty much hates men, you know? How'd he even, like, talk to her about it?"

"That day outside The Tea Cozy a couple of weeks ago," Judy said. "It had to have been then. Remember, Susannah, she was out there for awhile after I came in? She said she was giving him a piece of her mind. But maybe she wasn't. Maybe she heard him telling me I was in a perfect position to help him pull off some really great new scam and she decided to help him out herself."

"She wasn't out there that long," Susannah reminded her. "Maybe ten, twelve minutes, maximum."

"They could have made a date to meet later and iron out the details."

"But why?" Susannah said, trying to understand. "Why would she do it?"

"Why does anybody usually do something like that?" Matt put his hand on her knee and squeezed it comfortingly. "Money."

Judy snorted rudely. "If she thought she was going to make any money working with Eddie, she was crazy. He barely gives his girls enough to live on."

"Do you think she, like, knew the place was going to be raided?" Heather asked. "I mean, she was supposed to be helping out at the party like usual. But she went home sick instead, you know?"

Matt smiled a bit evilly. "I think what probably made her sick was hearing Susannah and me arguing in her office about the investigation."

"Poor Helen," Susannah said.

Matt laughed softly. "Susannah, sweetheart, she was using your business to sell sex. Making appointments to send teenage girls like Heather to men's hotel rooms. How can you say 'poor Helen'?"

But it wasn't really a question. He knew perfectly well how she could: it was just the way she was. And, God help him, he loved her that way.

"We've got to help her," Susannah said.

"We'll make sure she has a lawyer waiting for her at the police station when they bring her in," Matt said soothingly.

"The police are going to arrest her?"

Matt nodded. "Of course they're going to arrest her. She's committed a crime. Or, at least, been an accessory to one. As soon as the police find out she's involved, they're going to want to bring her in for questioning."

"How are they going to find out she's involved?" Susannah asked, but she knew the answer.

"Because I'm going to tell them," Matt said. "I'm an officer of the court," he added before she could say anything. "I've taken a sworn oath to uphold the law. By not telling what I know, I'd be guilty of withholding information in a criminal investigation."

"I'm not asking you to withhold information," Susannah said earnestly. "I wouldn't do that. But couldn't you just sort of delay it for a little while?"

"Define 'a little while,'" Matt said dryly.

"Not long. Maybe just a couple of hours? Just long enough for her to turn herself in? The police and the people at the DA.'s office look favorably on people who turn themselves in, don't they?"

Matt nodded. "All right. But if she hasn't turned herself in by nine o'clock in the morning, I'm going to send two uniforms after her."

She leaned over and pressed a kiss to his cheek. "Thank you, Matt," she said warmly, then stood, looking down at him expectantly.

"Are we going someplace?" he asked, although he already knew the answer.

"Helen's going to need friends to help her through this," Susannah said, as if it made perfect sense that she—the wronged party—should be that friend. "And a lawyer."

THE SMALL HOUSE in the Sunset district of San Francisco looked like every other neat, pastel-colored row house in the city's fog belt. The only indication that it might be any different were the lights blazing from every window, cutting through the curling fog to send lozenges of light spilling out onto the street.

"Well, we know she's up, at least," Matt said, as he turned his Lincoln onto the concrete apron of her driveway and killed the engine. "I'd say that probably means she knows the gig is up."

"I hope she's all right," Susannah fretted as they mounted the steps to the front porch.

Matt shook his head. "Leave it to you to feel sympathy for someone who may have done serious damage to your livelihood," he said, but it wasn't really a criticism.

Susannah shushed him with a look and rang the doorbell.

There was nothing but silence from inside.

She raised her hand and pounded on the door. "Helen? Are you in there? Helen? It's Susannah Bennington."

There was a fumbling noise on the other side of the door. "Susannah?"

"Yes, Helen, it's me." She looked up at Matt. "I've brought Matt Ryan with me. You're going to need his help."

There was a moment's silence, and then the sound of a dead bolt being thrown back and a chain being unlatched. The door opened a crack.

"Are you all right, Helen?" Susannah asked. "Can we come in?"

Helen nodded hesitantly and then stepped back, pulling the door open so they could enter. It was obvious she'd been crying. Her eyes were red and swollen, her skin blotchy.

"Do you mind if I take that?" Matt said, indicating the two-foot length of pipe clutched in her right hand.

Helen looked down at the pipe, as if she'd been unaware that she was holding it. "I thought you might be that horrible Eddie Devine," she said, making no move to hand over the pipe. "He's called me twice tonight, threatening me. He said if I told anyone about our arrangement, he'd see that I regretted it."

"He won't be threatening anyone for a while." Matt reached out to take the length of pipe from her. He placed it in the umbrella stand. "As of an hour ago, he's in jail."

"Jail?" Helen said hesitantly. And then her face crumbled. "Oh, God! I'm going to jail, too, aren't I? I'm going to be a jailbird!"

"No. No, it won't be that bad," Susannah said, reaching out to comfort her. "You won't be a jailbird."

"Oh, Susannah, I'm sorry. I'm so sorry. I never meant for this to happen. I—"

"Hush," Susannah said. "It's going to be all right. I promise. Everything will be all right. Matt will take care of everything."

Matt sighed, resigning himself to playing the white knight—probably for the rest of his life—and waited until the older woman got herself under control. "Mrs. Sanford," he said when she'd calmed down, "are you ready to talk now?"

"Yes." She straightened and looked up at him, still dabbing at her eyes with the tissue Susannah had pressed into her hand. "Yes, of course." She looked back and forth between Matt and Susannah. "You want to know why I did it, don't you?"

"If you feel up to telling us," Susannah said.

"I needed the money," she admitted. "It's as simple and awful as that. Everybody thinks I got a big settlement in the divorce. That Donald was forced to provide for me because of how long we'd been married and the adultery and everything. But divorce doesn't work that way anymore. I got the house and half of our savings. What was left of our savings," she amended with a sniff. "He'd spent most of what we had on that girlfriend of his. He ran up a lot of credit-card bills, too. Bills that the judge said he was supposed to pay but he hasn't. The collection agencies have been calling me, threatening to take my house. So when I heard Eddie Devine telling Judy he had a scheme where she could make some 'real' money and that she wouldn't have to turn tricks to do it, well—" she lifted her plump shoulders in an uneasy shrug and looked away "—I listened. And then, when she made it clear to him that she wasn't interested and wouldn't do it, no matter what, I told him I would." Fresh tears of shame welled up. "And I did. I'm sorry, Susannah. I was sorry the very first day

I got involved. But it was too late by then—I'd said yes. And Eddie wouldn't let me change my mind. Even when everything started to go so wrong, he kept insisting it would work."

"You're going to have to provide a few more details when we take you down to the police station so you can turn yourself in," Matt said when she fell silent.

"Turn myself in?"

"The police will be more lenient than if you wait to be arrested," Susannah told her. "It's really just a formality."

"It's more than a mere formality," Matt corrected her, believing honesty was the best policy in a case like this. "The detectives assigned to the case will interrogate you," Matt said to Helen. "They'll want to know how you got involved with Eddie Devine, what your arrangement with him was and how it worked, how long it's been in operation. They'll want names if you have them. That sort of thing. I suggest you cooperate fully and completely. It will be much easier on you if you do."

"Oh, I will," Helen said fervently. "I'll tell them everything I know."

"What happens after that depends on your answers to those questions. Since I'm with the D.A.'s office, I'll have some prosecutorial discretion as to whether, or for what, you're charged."

"He'll arrange it so you don't have to spend any time in jail," Susannah said. "You'll be able to come right back home."

"I'll *try*," Matt affirmed with a rebuking look at Susannah. "But I can't promise anything. A lot depends on your answers to the detectives' questions."

Helen nodded. "I understand."

"Get your coat, then," Matt said gently, "and we'll go."

"I THINK EVERYTHING went pretty well, don't you?" Susannah said as she and Matt drove away from the police station. It was five-fifteen a.m. and the city was quiet, the nearly deserted streets blanketed in early-morning fog.

"Nobody had the book thrown at them, if that's what you mean," Matt said. "Except Eddie Devine," he added with a note of satisfaction in his voice.

With the details Helen Sanford had provided, they had enough to put Eddie Devine away for a good long time.

"Judy was right about him, you know," Matt said. "It was incredibly stupid of him to try to use The Personal Touch." He shook his head. "There was no way it would have ever worked. Hell, according to what Helen said, the whole scheme was so poorly thought-out it started to fall apart from the first day."

"What will happen to Helen now?"

"She'll get immunity for testifying against Eddie."

"No jail time?"

"No jail time," Matt assured her. "But she will be on probation."

Susannah reached over and touched his hand where it lay on the steering wheel. "Have I told you yet how wonderful you've been through all of this?"

"No," he said, glancing away from the road for a moment to smile at her. "Tell me now."

"You're a knight in shining armor," Susannah said, meaning it sincerely. "My hero. I don't know what I would have done without you."

"Does that mean you'll marry me?" His tone was teasing but the question was deadly serious.

Susannah laughed softly. "After all this, you *still* want to marry me?"

"Still," Matt affirmed. "Always."

Susannah felt her heart leap in her chest, joy like a wild thing trying to break free. She reined it in, ruthlessly. One of them had to be practical; the irony wasn't lost on her that that one was her.

"What about your campaign?" she said. "Your family tradition of public service? Following in your father's footsteps? None of that will be possible if you marry me."

"Says who?"

"Matt, be reasonable. You know I'm ri—"

"I'm sick and tired of being reasonable," Matt said forcefully. "I've been reasonable all my life. I've done everything that's expected of me. What's required. What's sensible. Well, this is one time I am definitely *not going to be reasonable, dammit!*"

He turned the Lincoln into his driveway as he uttered the last words, braking so hard that Susannah's seat belt locked, snapping her back against the seat.

"My feelings for you aren't reasonable, Susannah."

He slammed the gearshift into *Park* and killed the engine.

"They never have been, not since the first day I met you."

He released his seat belt and reached out to release Susannah's, too.

"And I'm not a reasonable man when I'm around you," he said, dragging her across the leather seat and into his arms. "I'm not practical. Or rational. Hell, I'm not even *sane!*" he growled furiously, and crushed his mouth to hers.

Susannah's response was as explosive as if she were a keg of dynamite and his kiss a burning match. She locked her arms around his neck like a vise, holding him as closely, as tightly, as he was holding her. Their mouths plundered recklessly, their lips open wide, their tongues engaged in a heated, sensual duel where both combatants came out winners.

He was hard and hot.

She was soft and wet.

They were both breathing hard, aching with intemperate need and a heedless, reckless passion that drove them to find the surcease that came only in each other's arms.

"Say you want me," Matt demanded savagely, dragging his mouth down the slender column of her neck.

"I want you."

"Say you love me."

"I love you," Susannah moaned, gasping as he pushed back the trench coat out of the way and nipped her bare shoulder in a blatant act of possession.

He moved his hands to her head, threading his fingers through her hair, holding her head tilted back so he could gaze deeply into her eyes. Piercing, peerless blue stared into eyes as soft and warm as bubbling chocolate. Searching endlessly. Beseeching sweetly. Finding passion. And need. And a love so deep and strong it couldn't be denied.

"Say you'll marry me," Matt whispered.

"I'll marry you," Susannah whispered back.

He smiled.

And she smiled.

He gentled his hands in her hair, cupping the curve of her head between them, and brought her lips to his. The kiss was tender this time. Soft. Sweet. Endlessly beguiling. Smiling lips pressed to smiling lips. Silken tongue tips delicately exploring. Fingertips dancing over a stubbled jaw and a satin throat, tracing the whorl of a dainty earlobe and the hard curve of a Nordic cheekbone. They sighed and murmured, nuzzled and nestled, fondled and caressed and cuddled joyously, wordlessly expressing the wonder and magic of being in love.

"The windows are fogged up," Susannah murmured when Matt finally freed her mouth.

"Hmm?" he said, his lips pressed against the soft skin of her throat.

"The windows. They're fogged up."

Matt opened his eyes to look. "So they are." He lifted his head to grin at her. "The last time that happened, I was in the back seat of my dad's car with the head cheerleader. Cami, I think her name was."

Susannah raised an expressive eyebrow. "Would you like to re-experience your heedless youth and climb into the back seat now?"

Matt twisted a bit to glance over his shoulder. "It's very tempting," he said, after a moment's consideration. "But I'm not seventeen anymore—thank God— and there's a perfectly good king-size bed in the house."

Susannah stuck her bottom lip out in a pout. "No sense of adventure," she teased.

"You're looking for adventure?"

Susannah smiled her witchy smile.

Matt grinned and adjusted their position on the front seat, pushing her down beneath him. She felt his hand skim up her leg, up under her dress, reaching for the moist delta between her thighs.

She caught at it, stopping him before he reached his goal. "It's six o'clock in the morning," she reminded him. "And we're parked in your driveway. Anyone could walk by and see us. Some eager beaver reporter might decide he has one more question he wants answered."

"What happened to that wild sense of adventure?"

"Well, really," she said primly. "One of us has to be reasonable."

Epilogue

Ten years later
Sacramento, California

"WE COULDN'T ASK for a more perfect day for a swearing-in ceremony, could we?" the news commentator asked his co-anchor as the scene that filled television screens all over California gave proof to his words. "The temperature is a balmy seventy-two degrees on this winter's day. There's a light breeze out of the West. Governor-Elect Matthew Ryan is at the podium. His wife Susannah Bennington Ryan has just been handed the Bible to hold while he takes the oath of office."

"Oh, look," enthused the female co-anchor, "their two children are going to share the honor. Ben Ryan is eight years old. His little sister Milly is almost six," she informed the television audience as they watched Susannah gather her children to her, lowering the Bible until they could each place a hand under it. "Although there's been no official word as yet, it's rumored that Mrs. Ryan is expecting the couple's third child sometime next summer. This will be the first time we've had children living in the governor's mansion in quite a few years. It will be quite a change—"

"How do they find out about that stuff?" Susannah groused, punching the remote control to pick up the evening news on another channel. "We haven't even announced it to the family yet."

"Well, look at it this way," Matt said, grinning at his disgruntled wife. "Now we won't have to."

"Matthew Ryan's first run for office ended in scandal when his then-fiancée Susannah Bennington was arrested in connection with a prostitution ring." The newscaster's voice ran over old file footage of Susannah's arrest and Matt's statement to the press when he ended his campaign for district judge. "The charges were later dismissed, but—"

"Oh, please," Susannah said, punching the remote again. "There were never any charges filed and there wasn't any scandal. You quit the campaign because you didn't want to be a district judge. Didn't anybody listen to your speech?"

". . . and doesn't Mrs. Ryan look stunning? The unusual lapel pin she's wearing is one of a kind, made especially for her by the young California designer Heather Lloyd. Ms. Lloyd is a long-time personal friend of the Ryans—"

"Heather said she's already been swamped with orders," Susannah said gleefully. "I told her to just wait until everyone sees the gorgeous earrings she designed to go with my inaugural gown."

"Shouldn't you be getting into that inaugural gown?" Matt asked, passing between his wife and the television set on his way to the bathroom to shave.

Susannah glanced up at him from her seat on the edge of the bed. "Not until just before we're ready to leave," she said, and pushed the remote control again. "I don't want to wrinkle it."

"During his two terms on the City Council, Matthew Ryan was no stranger to controversy, even within his own home. An outspoken advocate of programs for women and children, gay rights and gun control, Mrs. Ryan was often heard voicing opinions contrary to those of her husband. During the summer of—"

Susannah clicked the remote control.

"The Ryan-Bennington marriage appears to be one of strange bedfellows—"

"Who's he calling strange?" Susannah demanded loudly, forgetting that she had once said the very same thing about their relationship. "You or me?"

"Got to be you," her loving husband hollered from the bathroom.

Click.

"...although having a strong-willed, outspoken wife doesn't seem to have hurt Matt Ryan's political career with the women voters of the State, political analysts say that on a national level it—"

Click.

"Don't you care what the political analysts have to say about my career?"

"Every one of them says something different and, so far, they've all been wrong."

"... Governor-Elect Matthew Ryan has just placed his hand on the Bible...."

"Why don't you turn that thing off?" Matt said, as he came out of the bathroom. "You've watched the swearing-in at least a dozen times already."

"It's a terrific ceremony," Susannah said, her eyes still on the television screen. "You look so noble. So dedicated. So gubernatorial." She gave him a slanted, sideways glance, her gaze raking down his long, well-formed body as he stood there beside the bed freshly showered and shaved. She raised an eyebrow. "If they could only see you now."

Matt looked down at himself. "What? Blue boxer shorts aren't gubernatorial?"

"Maybe we should get you some with the State Seal printed on them."

"The State Seal, huh?" He frowned. "I don't know abo—" He broke off as he caught her smile.

He eyed her consideringly. "Is there something about California's State Seal that turns you on?"

She shook her head. "There's something about California's governor that turns me on."

Matt reached out a long arm, pulling her off the bed and into his arms. "Have you ever wondered what it would be like to make love on the floor of the governor's mansion?"

"Right now?" Susannah raised her eyebrows in a patently false expression of shock as she leaned into his embrace. "When we're supposed to be getting ready for your Inaugural Ball?"

Matt's broad chest lifted in a theatrical sigh. "Maybe you're right," he said craftily, and made as if to loosen his embrace. "There probably isn't enough time."

Susannah tightened her arms around her husband's neck and smiled a slow, witchy smile, the one that challenged and invited at the same time. "We'll make time," she said as they sank down to the carpeted floor. "Kiss me."

Temptation

Lost Loves

'Right Man...Wrong time'

All women are haunted by a lost love—a disastrous first romance, a brief affair, a marriage that failed.

A second chance with him...could change everything.

Lost Loves, a powerful, sizzling mini-series from Temptation continues in April 1995 with...

**Even Cowboys Get the Blues
by Carin Rafferty**

MILLS & BOON

This month's
irresistible novels from

THE PERSONAL TOUCH by Candace Schuler

Lawyer Matt Ryan hadn't anticipated falling for the owner of a
classy dating service. And when rumours started that the
service was a front for criminal activity, he knew that
Susannah could be very dangerous—both for his career and his
heart…

BABY BLUES by Kristine Rolofson

When single mother Anne Winston returned to her home town
with her daughter, she was shocked to learn that sexy Chris
Bogart had moved back, too. He was about to learn that he was
a father. But could they become a family?

THE RETURN OF CAINE O'HALLORAN by JoAnn Ross

Lost Loves mini-series

Ten years ago, Caine and Nora had married because she was
pregnant—but their son's death tore apart their fragile union.
Since then Caine had experienced fame and glory, but now he
wanted more—Nora. Could he win her back?

C.J.'S DEFENCE by Carolyn Andrews

Successful attorney Roarke Farrell was determined to strip
away the sexy little suits opposing attorney C.J. Parker wore in
court—and to tear down the defences around her heart! *And*
he'd knock a hole in her legal defence a mile wide!

Spoil yourself next month
with these four novels from

EVEN COWBOYS GET THE BLUES by Carin Rafferty

Lost Loves mini-series

Tanner Chapel wanted his ex-wife back so bad it hurt. As far
as Annie cared, Tanner could take his guitar and…get lost. If
only he wasn't still the damned sexiest cowboy around!

STAR by Janice Kaiser

Five years ago, beautiful Hollywood movie star, Dina Winters,
broke her wedding plans to pursue an irresistible role. But had
she ever got over Michael? Now the two former lovers were
working together again and the sparks were about to fly.

COOPER'S LAST STAND by Hillary Hunter

Jed Cooper had lied his way into Ashley Jamieson's life, loved
her and then left her. He was the very worst person to have
around. But he was also the only man who could save her.

HER FAVOURITE HUSBAND by Leandra Logan

She had a different man for every night of the week! Madeline
Clancy ran her agency Just Like a Wife very smoothly. Until
she met her Friday man, Trey Turner. First he tried to pick her
up. Then he fired her! And then he begged her to pretend to be
his wife. How could a girl say no?

GET 4 BOOKS
AND A MYSTERY GIFT

Return the coupon below and we'll send you 4 Temptations absolutely FREE! We'll even pay the postage and packing for you.

We're making you this offer to introduce you to the benefits of Reader Service: FREE home delivery of brand-new Temptations, at least a month before they are available in the shops, FREE gifts and a monthly Newsletter packed with information.

Accepting these FREE books places you under no obligation to buy, you may cancel at any time, even after receiving just your free shipment. Simply complete the coupon below and send it to:

HARLEQUIN MILLS & BOON, FREEPOST, PO BOX 70, CROYDON CR9 9EL. ✂

- -

Yes, please send me 4 Temptations and a mystery gift as explained above. Please also reserve a subscription for me. If I decide to subscribe I shall receive 4 superb new titles every month for just £7.80* postage and packing free. I understand that I am under no obligation whatsoever. I may cancel or suspend my subscription at any time simply by writing to you, but the free books and gift will be mine to keep in any case.
I am over 18 years of age.

> **NO STAMP NEEDED**

1EP5T

Ms/Mrs/Miss/Mr _____

Address _____

_____

_____ Postcode _____

mps MAILING PREFERENCE SERVICE

Paperback Writer...

Have you got what it takes?

To celebrate 10 years of Temptation we are giving away a host of tempting prizes...

10 prizes of FREE Temptation Books for a whole year

— plus —

10 runner up prizes of *Thorntons* delicious Temptations Chocolates

Enter our Temptation Wordsearch Quiz Today and Win!

10th All you have to do is complete the wordsearch puzzle below and send it to us by 31 May 1995.

The first 10 correct entries drawn from the bag will each win 12 month's free supply of exciting Temptation books (4 books every month with a total annual value of around £100).

The second 10 correct entries drawn will each win a 200g box of *Thorntons* Temptations chocolates.

I	F	G	N	I	T	I	C	X	E
A	O	X	O	C	A	I	N	S	S
N	O	I	T	A	T	P	M	E	T
N	B	V	E	N	R	Y	N	X	E
I	R	O	A	M	A	S	N	Y	R
V	C	M	T	I	U	N	N	F	U
E	O	H	U	O	T	M	V	E	T
R	N	X	U	R	E	Y	S	I	N
S	L	S	M	A	N	F	L	Y	E
A	T	O	N	U	T	R	X	L	V
R	U	O	M	U	H	I	A	A	D
Y	W	D	Y	O	F	I	M	K	A

TEMPTATION
SEXY
FUN
EXCITING
TENTH

ROMANTIC
SENSUOUS
ADVENTURE
HUMOUR
ANNIVERSARY

PLEASE TURN
OVER FOR
ENTRY
DETAILS

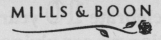

MILLS & BOON

HOW TO ENTER

10th All the words listed overleaf below the wordsearch puzzle, are hidden in the grid. You can find them by reading the letters forward, backwards, up and down, or diagonally. When you find a word, circle it or put a line through it.

Don't forget to fill in your name and address in the space below then put this page in an envelope and post it today (you don't need a stamp). Closing date 31st May 1995.

Temptation Wordsearch,
FREEPOST,
P.O. Box 344,
Croydon,
Surrey
CR9 9EL

COMP395

Are you a Reader Service Subscriber?   Yes ☐   No ☐

Ms/Mrs/Miss/Mr _____

Address _____

_____

_____ Postcode _____

One application per household. You may be mailed with other offers from other reputable companies as a result of this application.
Please tick box if you would prefer
not to share in these opportunities.   ☐